T0267469

A SECOND CHANCE ON EARTH

JUAN VIDAL

HOLIDAY HOUSE · NEW YORK

Library of Congress Cataloging-in-Publication Data

Names: Vidal, Juan, 1981- author.
Title: A second chance on earth / by Juan Vidal.
Description: First edition. | New York : Holiday House, 2024. | Audience:
  Ages 14 and up. | Audience: Grades 10—12. | Summary: "When
  sixteen-year-old Marcos travels to Cartagena, Colombia to scatter his
  late father's ashes, he strikes up a friendship with Camilo, a boy his
  age who works as a local taxi driver and shares Marcos' love for the
  novel One Hundred Years of Solitude"— Provided by publisher.
Identifiers: LCCN 2024000409 | ISBN 9780823457113 (hardcover)
Subjects: CYAC: Novels in verse. | Grief—Fiction. | Friendship—Fiction.
  Books and reading—Fiction. | Cartagena (Colombia)—Fiction. | LCGFT:
  Novels in verse.
Classification: LCC PZ7.5.V53 Se 2024 | DDC [Fic]—dc23
LC record available at https://lccn.loc.gov/2024000409

ISBN: 978-0-8234-5711-3 (hardcover)

"I PUT IT DOWN ON PAPER AND THEN THE GHOST DOES NOT ACHE SO MUCH."

—SANDRA CISNEROS

A QUIET WAR RAGES WITHIN

Nonstop at my mind's door.
A clash between
what I know is true

and something like denial.
Time slips
and I war on.

Some days I move through life numb,
convincing myself Papi is around the corner,
under the bed, over in the next room.

Other times, I wake in a panic,
reminded of death
in the dead of night.

I jump out of bed.
It hits me that Papi is gone.
That he will soon be one with the earth.

THE DAY IT WENT DOWN

felt like the wheels
came off. My world
broken and split
from all sides.

The largest shadow cast.
As if the sun had gone black
and the moon blood-red.

A hurricane barreling down
on all I love. The universe itself

handing out its worst,
and in a big, bad hurry.

Like you drew from a cursed
deck of cards and now

    you're a house in flames.

SCREAM THERAPY

Occasionally,
every so often,
if I get the sudden urge,

I'll push
out a roar when
there's an empty house.

An ear-splitting
scream, or maybe
two, or three.

The kind like
fractured bones or getting
fingers caught in the car door.

It is directed at no one and
absolutely everyone.
I do it for the hell of it.

For the rush.
Urgent as the tone
of the medic

as he says
I'm sorry, boy. I'm so sorry.
The sound of loss.

There's a trapped lion
alive and raging
inside my lungs.

EVERYTHING REMINDS ME OF WHAT I LOST

Fathers and sons
everywhere; here,
there, and around the way.
Reminding me that
father and son
is a thing
I once knew
like

weekends at the water park

smiling for no reason

piggyback rides

living-room sparring sessions

and

Papi's hair that smelled
like bread and coconut oil.

WHEN I WAS TWELVE

and having bad nightmares,
Papi told me about a thing
called lucid dreaming.
He called it *the magic of being aware*
you're dreaming while you're asleep.

My brain would travel to these dark places
where people I loved got sick or died,
making it hard for me to catch z's
because I was scared.
Scared all the time.

Papi owned this dreaming book.
It was slender, blue, and falling apart,
had helped him go *adventuring*
when he was younger
so he could be *emotionally*
and mentally present in his dreams.

I didn't want all that
gibberish.
I simply wished
for the nightmares
to stop and never come back.
We read about the MILD technique,
the Mnemonic Induction to Lucid Dreaming.

What you do is you repeat
the same phrase to yourself
as you lie down.
Something like,
I know this is all a dream.
Over and over
until you're out like a light.

And it worked.
The spells
went away.

I was cured.
Healed, delivered.
Papi was hailed as a genius.

But even he was stunned,
and we all laughed and howled
about how this hippie-dippie
hocus-pocus
worked like a flipping charm.

A few years later,
the worst horror came true.
Truer than true.
And I still haven't
fully woken up.
Slim chance I ever will.
But I don't want to think this way.

MY ART TEACHER MRS. RIVAS

told me the five stages of grief are

denial, anger, bargaining,

depression, acceptance.

I can't say where I fall

on this spectrum but she

asked me to draw how I feel,

if I felt up to it. I made a doodle

of a fish washed up on shore,

dry as a bone.

THIS OR THAT

Maybe grief is a fish out of water.
  Maybe grief is a thing with wings.
    Maybe grief is doubts that keep piling.
      Maybe grief is the prison of your mind.
        Maybe grief is a thought you can't express.
          Maybe grief is a meaningless idea.
            A poem shaped like stairs when you'd prefer an elevator.

MA SAYS IT WAS PAPI'S APPETITE FOR LIFE

How he memorized poems,
and loved to eat well,
and sing badly,
and dance merengue
that won her over.
Papi used to tell me stories.
Long and sometimes silly stories
about his coming up near the coast.

His days spent swimming,
chasing girls,
and finding

all kinds of trouble.

Papi shirtless in our kitchen,
cooking up a storm.
Moving slowly to a bolero
or wild and fast to
bongos and 12-string guitars.

Watch this, he'd say,
and slide across the floor
like he was a part of the circus.

Side to side,
spinning like a bottle top.
My little sister Daniela just stared,
her coffee eyes wide with shock.

You're weird, she said,
without using words.
He might let up to stir the beans
or flip the pork chops
on the hot stove,
but he never stopped dancing.

Always
dancing.

One hand over his heart
as if he were reciting
the pledge.
His feet tap-tapping
on the ground.

Papi going on
like there was no
tomorrow,
until eventually *poof*
there wasn't one.
Not for him.

STORIES LIKE RIVERS

I'm told
the old stories
live on inside me.
Run like rivers
through my veins,
even if I don't have
a father around
to tell me
any new ones.
And so I
hold tight to
those I've collected
over the years,
keep them
close to the
chest like old birds
keep silver and gold.
I guess that
makes me some
kind of a hoarder.
But instead of
precious metals,

I'm a hoarder of
tales and anecdotes
I hope to never lose.

Because if I do,
    then what?

What happens to a story
lost, or misplaced?
    Does it disappear,
like an old sock?

And what happens
to the person
a story is *about?*
Do they cease to exist
after we've stopped
passing around their stories?

AFTER PAPI PASSED, I STARTED

writing in secret.
I've never shared
this with anyone.
It all began with:

me curious,
me mopey and depressed,
rooting through Papi's
bookshelves one afternoon
looking for a dictionary

so I could find
the word *contusion.*

(It means: a region of injured tissue or skin in which
blood capillaries have been ruptured; a bruise.)

I was just trying to learn more
about Papi's brain injury,
but then,
I noticed another book.

This one had a neon-green cover that caught my attention.
I picked it up and read the words
ONE HUNDRED YEARS OF SOLITUDE.

Also on the cover:

birds and a snake,
a fairy and ferns.

A woman that looked like she was
glowing in a deep forest.

The name Gabriel García Márquez.

I skimmed the pages
and the more I read
the stranger things got.

Soon it was all
ghosts and golden fish,

prophetic curses,
and plagues of insomnia.

Made my arms tingle.
The words felt
sweet on my lips
as I read them
aloud in the still,
almost-black of the room.

It wasn't like the poetry
or the fables
we read in school—
this was weirder,

you could even say darker.
I wouldn't call it that myself,
but you could say it.

I started devouring it,
breezing through 10 to 15
pages a night after dinner
or in the early a.m. before toast.

. . . time was not passing . . . it was turning in a circle . . .

That's how it felt after Papi
was taken from us.
First, like the days
were getting away from me,
soaring past in beams of light.

But after some weeks,
time grew heavy,
weighing me down
like wet denim
hanging on a clothesline.

So, I scribbled
in a notepad.
Trying to make sense
of what I was feeling.
I thought that maybe, *maybe,*
I could write well in my own way.

Maybe I could write poems,
or whatever you want to call it,
about what it's like to miss your hero
who is now ashes and can't
tell you any more stories.

I COULD WRITE ABOUT WANTING TO LEAVE

the only home I have known.

To go
where I could feel

him

in his own country.
Away from Miami,
that city I love.

That city of a zillion and one names.
That loony.
That loud.
That constant summer
that sticks to you
like gym shorts
on sweaty skin.

A THING ABOUT POETRY

is that you can write what you want,

in whatever language you choose,

with whatever instrument you have.

The one thing that matters,

the single requirement,

the only reason worth bothering

with poetry in the first place,

is to leave the blank page better

than it was before you found it.

INTERROGATION

Do I have enough language?

 Can I find the necessary words . . .

to

fully

express

a

wound?

PAPI'S POEM I FOUND WRITTEN ON A WAFFLE HOUSE NAPKIN GOES . . .

If there's any villain
in this life, it is not the

debt collectors
serial killers
bullies
compulsive liars
animal abusers
dictators
thieves
cannibals
drunk drivers

slow walkers
big talkers
false prophets
complainers
the wicked,
power-hungry
governments
with greedy plans
or even the people
who clap when the plane lands . . .

no, the real villain in the story is life itself,
the beauty
the cruelty
the randomness . . .

but mostly how quickly it is over.

PAPI LOVED

writers & prizefighters & nail-biters & all-nighters & hamburger
sliders at hole-in-the-wall diners & Clint Eastwood in *Pale Rider*
& highlighters & the tats on bikers & survivors & early risers &
catching spiders & recliners & providers & deep-sea divers &
tigers & mountain climbers & apple cider & movies with subtitles
& daily reminders & hitchhikers & the Dolphins versus the 49ers
& how Jesus called the hypocrites of his day *a brood of vipers*

   & best of all

Papi loved finding the right words.

HAVE YOU EVER

encountered a book or story that
KO'd you, Iron Mike Tyson style?

A book or story that made
you ponder if every other book

or story ever written or told
was even *good*?

A book or story that hit you
square in the face
and heart like some
abracadabra casting a hex

from an unknown planet?
Me neither. Or, correction:
not until now.
Not until
ONE HUNDRED YEARS OF SOLITUDE.

IN MIAMI

we live in
an apartment

on the second floor
of a building

where it's hardly ever quiet.
A building where drums shake the spackled walls

and salsa music fills the air.
Three and four kids to a room.

Where grandparents, aunts, and uncles live stuffed together
like trying to squeeze balloons into a dresser drawer.

A building where on Saturday mornings the smell
of fried eggs and salami takes over.

If you're there in the afternoon or night
it's the aroma of a seven-meat stew.

The crackle and pop of peppers sautéing
two doors down.

Where children run berserk and old folks
sit outside on lawn chairs drinking beer

and laughing
with their whole body.

Some cooking or jabbering on the steps.
Daniela and her bout-to-be-freshmen crew
blabbering about

classmates they like or about
how little Raquel from up there

on 3rd Street got knocked up by an older boy.
Someone yelling that their Huffy got stolen.

Where's my bike?!
Who took my bike?!

Somebody's grandpa inside
watching the Heat game.

Shoot the ball, you fool!
¡Tira la pelota, imbécil!

I'VE BEEN SHOOTING HOOPS

pretty much every day
for the last month.

To help me cope, I guess.
Like how after a friend from school

lost his mom to cancer
he started training jiu-jitsu

to free his mind,
so to speak. He showed me how

to do a rear-naked choke
and something called a Kimura,

a double-joint armlock that leaves
your opponent squirming and defenseless.

AFTER THE FUNERAL

After the tears
and the speeches,
after the prayers
and heavenly blessings
at the corner church,

I went up the block
with the rock tucked
in the crook of my arm.
Still dressed in my suit.

Shot around for a while
in a daze
until the idea struck me to play
Around the World.

You know the game.
If I sunk a basket,
I moved to the next line.

If I missed, I started over.
I got it in my bone head
to try and make it to the opposite
end of the key and back again
without missing once
or even touching the rim.
Do you have any clue
how difficult that is?

That's 9 straight swishes one way.
18 total nothing-but-nets,
if you're keeping count.
Wouldn't let myself
go home until I did it.

Shot after shot,
worn out in the blazing sun.

I've been perfecting my stroke
against the pain of this new reality.

A sweet jump shot
and no pops to show it off to.

THE PATRON SAINT OF BROKEN PROMISES

Papi used to:

Promise me
I would never be without a father

Promise me
he would never leave Ma

Promise me
he would teach me to dance

Promise me
I would learn to drive a stick shift

Promise me
he would take us back to Joshua Tree National Park

Promise me
I would be able to talk to him about anything, anytime

Promise me
he would show me how to ride a motorcycle

Promise me
I would he would I would he would.

THIS SUMMER WAS ABOUT TO BE A DRAG

Why? Because Devon and Hector up and left.
Both gone, good as ghost.

Each of them having their fun
miles from home. Miles from the 305.

Devon running around in Jamaica with cousins,
Hector in gator-infested Orlando

for soccer camp,
gone mad weeks.

Most of the summer, according to my math.
Math isn't my jam but I know that much.

I will basically be in Miami alone.
Alone with my thoughts.

Have some basketball games lined up,
but I'm not close with anyone on the team.

I'm the only solid player out of eight of us,
which irks me to no end.

Jay is tall and can rebound,
but that's it.

Isaiah's got a half-decent jumper,
but can't dribble to save his soul.

That's the YMCA for you: a mix of kids
who want to be there,

and others that would rather
sit in front of a screen in pajamas

slamming buttons on a controller.
Sad. Sad. Triple sad.

If Devon and Hector had stuck around
we'd have dominated the league.

We'd have put every last one of those scrubs
to shame, dead on arrival.

BUT SOME GOOD NEWS IS THAT

Ma finally got me a phone.
I was using her old one and

am happy to report I
have now graduated to having
my own—complete with
an actual line
and phone number.

What happened is
that some Tuesday,
she forgot I was staying
at the Y late to ball.

When she didn't hear
from me for hours,
she went full frantic,
searching, scared,
calling around everywhere.
Embarrassing as all hell.

Call it paranoia.
Call it the love
of a mother bear.

In the end, she agreed
it was time.

Had I known
all I needed
to do to get a new
phone was to vanish
like a tube of Chapstick
for three hours

I'd have gotten myself
lost ages ago.

My boys Devon and Hector
both got lines
when they were twelve.
Their parents
are the chill type
who let their kids
duck out
a week before
the school year ends
for summer vacation.

Anyway, every time I wanted
to call them to talk NBA
or
school crushes,
I would have to use Ma's phone.
Not so great for a 16-year-old.

The first thing I did
with my new digits
was dial Hector,
who didn't answer.
Everyone knows you
don't pick up
from unknown numbers.

I texted *It's Marcos.*
He called back
and we talked
for 37 minutes.

I told Hector
about the terrible
players at the YMCA.
How if the three of us
were on the squad,
we'd be killing those
chumps quick-fast.

Seriously, I can
just picture it.

Through the legs.
Behind the back.
Buckets on buckets.

I've been best friends
with Devon and Hector
since the 6th grade.

They were already tight
before I came along
and made us a trio.
Sometimes we're the
Three Wise Men
and other times
the Three Blind Mice.

THE THING ABOUT DEVON

is that we're the same but different.
We share similar brain waves but physically are opposites.

Same: we both have a lonely side,
    we read books even outside of school
Different: I'm short-ish, he's one of the tallest in our grade

Same: we can be sarcastic, sometimes people think we're weird
Different: my skin is pecan brown, his is a shade darker

Same: both of us have lost a family member:
    me a father, him a twin sister
Different: my hands are normal size,
      he can palm a regulation basketball

Same: we like old school hip-hop and 90s martial arts movies
Different: I had some acne last year, his face is smooth as silk

Same: we're both dreamers, we have a habit of drifting off
    into our own worlds
Different: I prefer Nike, he mostly wears Adidas

Same: in 8th grade, we both had crushes
    on girls who didn't like us back in that way
Different: I'm a Pisces, he's a Capricorn

Same: we got into aliens after watching
    a documentary about Area 51
Different: I have long, wild hair, he keeps a short high fade

HECTOR

is the ambitious one of the group.
He's more of a doer than a dreamer.

More of a planner than a procrastinator.
More of how I need to be sometimes.

It's no secret that Hector
is gifted when it comes to sports.
He's good at everything
from basketball to football,
skateboarding to ping-pong.
But where he shines the brightest,
and what he loves the best, is soccer.

He's like a young Cristiano Ronaldo
the way he keeps defenders guessing,
guarding the ball like it's
his mom's King James Bible.
I can see him now at camp,
eating everybody's breakfast, lunch, and dinner.

And while he's at it, their dessert too.

MORE ABOUT DEVON

He's like the brother
I wish I had,
the kind of brother I wish
Papi and Ma had given me.

He's also the kind of brother
that goes to the Caribbean
for way too long
when you need him most.

But you could argue
it's not his fault,
I'll give him that.
He's not the one to blame
for a planned family getaway.

I'll blame him anyway.

I CAN'T SAY FOR CERTAIN

but I believe I may have
just come across what can only
be described as a perfect sentence.
I know how nerdy that sounds,
and so be it.
I accidentally flipped
too far ahead in the novel
and BOOM, there it was . . .

Lost in the solitude of his immense power,
he began to lose direction.

I SAW THIS NEWS STORY

a few days after Papi died.

9-year-old New Jersey boy sneaks onto plane, flies to Puerto Rico

The headline flashed
across the muted television.

I sat in silence struggling
to comprehend how
that could happen.

It hit me that if Ma
would not take me and Daniela
to Colombia to feel closer to Papi
because she is busy
working at her hair salon job
to make bread
to keep us alive and fed, then
        maybe I could
get there myself.

It seemed impossible
but I knew it wasn't.
The proof that it could
be done was
there in front of me.
The proof of a successful crime.

9-year-old New Jersey boy sneaks onto plane, flies to Puerto Rico

I thought that if *I* did it,
the new headline would read:

16-year-old Miami boy sneaks onto plane, flies to Colombia
or
*Miami teen with no ticket boards flight to Cartagena to connect
        with dead father*

I would just have to
do it on a weekday,
and dodge three
levels of security.
TSA.
Gate agents.
Flight crew.

Ma wouldn't even know
I was missing
until my feet
were cool sunk in the ocean
and it was too late
to stop me.

Before I could
go through with it,
and believe me,
I had every
intention of doing so,
Ma announced that we'd be
traveling to Cartagena.

To return Papi
to the city he loved
more than any other.
The city he used to call
"sacred ground" with
a glint in his eye.
To pour him out
like a sacrifice.

It'll be good, she said.
We need this.

So much for my fantasy
of becoming a
full-fledged fugitive.
I'm sure I'll have another
chance or three
to pursue a life
of devious crime.
Prayer hands.

EASY BREEZY

When Papi reminisced
about Cartagena,
he made it feel
like a mix of sunshine
and rainbows
and rain pelting windows
and pounding roofs
rattling the whole world.

ALL MY LIFE

I've heard no shortage
of thoughts and opinions
about my parents' homeland.

From depictions in
movies and TV shows
to mumbo jumbo
from acquaintances
when they learn
that my family is from
where my family is from.

It's all ignorant as hell.
For some, Colombia
will always be drug smuggling
and the dangerous cartels
that made the rules for so long.

Massacres.
Kidnappings.
A man by the name
of Pablo Escobar.

For some, Colombia
will always be:
the 1980s
blood
guns
corrupt politicians
crooked cops
cocaine cowboys.

It will always be about
suffering so horrific
you thought the world
was going to end.

But I always knew
there is more to it.
I knew it from Papi
and his stories.
I knew it because no place
stays the same forever.
Just like no person
stays the same forever.

I SPENT THE FOLLOWING NIGHTS

lying in bed, fantasizing
about Colombia.

What it would be like,
smell like, taste like.
Would I fall head over heels
and never want to come back?

I created a sort of tropical
Narnia in my head.
A dreamlike world with
majestic mountains,
clear-as-glass water,
and an ongoing battle
of good versus evil.

A world that connected me
to everyone and everything
that made Papi who he was

and me who I am
but have yet to fully discover.

WHEN THE DAY ARRIVED

I was torn, split in two.

One side of me was

eager for the adventure

ahead, the other side

bitter and down that Papi could not

enjoy it with us. Ma carried

what is left of him in a brass urn

with leaves engraved on it.

Leaves of absence, I thought.

I WISH I COULD TELL

you an epic story.
I wish I could go
into detail about how my
making it to Cartagena
is the stuff of spy movies.

An elaborate operation
where I had to use
my magnificent powers
to become invisible
or
rely on some special set of skills
to slip through the cracks.

I wish I could tell you
some gripping nonfiction
about how I snuck onto a
439 Boeing aircraft
without a ticket—how
I evaded every obstacle,
and about how
my heart pounded
in my chest like the street
performers back home
who smash pots and pans
for dollars and
    change.

But I can't. Not yet.
The hopefully epic story starts after we land.

TODAY, I'M SURROUNDED

by the white sands,
blue-green waters,
and bright-colored houses
of Cartagena, Colombia.

We came to
scatter ashes.
To let go, as they say.
To close the page on
Papi, who was crushed
in a motorcycling accident

    almost one month ago now.

Ma tells me we've been here
on holiday twice,
or maybe three times.
But I was a rug-rat kid
and don't remember it none.

Cartagena,
where my folks are from.
Where they met
and stumbled
into love.

WE ARE WE ARE WE ARE

so happy
when we get off
the airplane.

Even more relieved
to feel the
Cartagena air
in our lungs.

Zoned out and oblivious
to airport traffic, I almost
get hit by a taxi, dropping my book
and face-planting on the pavement.

Aaaaaaaah,
ONE HUNDRED YEARS OF SOLITUDE,
the driver says

as he walks out
of his taxi to greet us
and help me stand up.

Thanks, I say,
my book on the concrete
but still intact.

The boy, who can't be too much
older than me, introduces
himself as Camilo. He is tall
and thin and sports blue jeans

and a Dream Team jersey,
number 15. That's Magic
Johnson if you're not aware.

Camilo had been circling
the terminal looking
for passengers who needed rides
to their destination.

Gabriel García Márquez
was born Sunday,
March 6, 1927

in the sleepy town of Aracataca.

A town of wooden shacks,
dusty air, and unpaved roads.

He came into the world
like any other.

Clinging to life,
soft as pan de yuca,
full of potential.

I notice a small dent
on the bumper of Camilo's taxi
and a beat-up copy of
ONE HUNDRED YEARS OF SOLITUDE
with a different cover sitting
on the dashboard.
I don't think much of it,
figure everyone here
probably owns one.
Makes sense.

MA GIVES CAMILO THE ADDRESS

to Papi's sister's place,
where we'll be staying,
and we're off
to the races.

The city is bursting
with energy and
so much to stare at:
famous cathedrals,
graffiti murals,
and rainbow streets.

When we pull up
to the house, Camilo hands
me an old receipt with his number
written on it. He offers to take me
on a tour of the area and talk more
about the author García Márquez.
Could you imagine?

AND SO HERE WE ARE

and here I am.
In a land
I do not know
but that looks
and feels
familiar still.

My tía Norma lives in
a pink house with blue windows
a stone's throw from the beach.

We're here to be together.
To remember the best man
we ever knew

and likely will ever know.
Most of me can't help but wish
I had come solo.

Ten toes in the sand,
instead
of forty.

FORTY TOES

represent a lot of
metaphorical baggage
to lug around.

If I had come solo,
I would wander
shopping plazas
and crowded squares.
Stopping only for cheap,
foreign-to-me munchies
and sugary drinks.
Too shy or thickheaded
like Papi to ask
for directions
as my mind
plays back
every memory
like a playlist on repeat.

I STRETCH OUT ON THE FLOOR

thinking about the young
taxi driver and his offer
as the women
swap stories about people
they used to know.

Something about Camilo,
his speech, or the vibe
he gave off reminds me
of someone I used
to know, too.

I hope I can take him up
on the invitation,

sooner rather than later.
Fingers crossed
Ma doesn't protest
or put up a fight.

LITTLE SISTER WATCHES

television, punching, clicking
until she lands
on the evening news.
It doesn't take long
for us to notice how
little they leave
to the imagination—
at least compared to
what we're used to.

In the span of minutes
we see a blood-soaked corpse
next to a dumpster
and a graphic segment
about a house fire. What really
gets us is the clip of two men

who'd been gored nasty
at a bullfighting festival
near the coast.
The bull's horn cut
through one man's heart
like a knife through butter.
The second, who tried to help,

died at the hospital
after bleeding out
from his wounds.

Daniela can't stand the sight.
I can't look away.
The image of a bull's horn
piercing a human organ
on basic cable
will never leave my head.
That's heartbreaking, I joke,
but nobody laughs.
Heart . . . breaking,
I say again, offering
them another opportunity
to appreciate my comedy.

SOMETIMES

dark
humor
is
not
the
way

I
repeat

sometimes
dark

humor
is
not
the
way.

THE RADIO

plays politics as I roll out
of bed in the morning.
It's 7:30 a.m. Too early for politics.
Tía, in leggings and a WrestleMania VII
tank top, waters and sings to her plants.
Chrysanthemums and dahlias, she says.
Her voice is light and bubbly,
like her song can help keep them
healthy. And maybe it can.

Tía, I ask, *how come you never got married?*
Ma looks at me like, *Boy, what is the matter with you?*

Tía begins: *I've been close a few times, it*
just never worked out. People change.
But your parents got lucky,
they found their perfect match.
Besides, I have my plants to keep me company.

The radio program cuts to a commercial.
The announcement of an upcoming musical
tour by the Colombian singer Juanes,

who tía confidently and excitedly calls
The Most Handsome Man in the World.

¡Qué chimba!, she says.

Then tía leans in to whisper,
shielding her mouth
so the plants can't hear:

Maybe I will marry Juanes.
These babies deserve a Papá
who can really serenade them.
What do you think?

Well, I say, *if somehow you end up*
getting hitched with Juanes, I know
just what to wear for the occasion.
Funeral suit same as my wedding suit.

SOMEBODY SHOULD BE KISSED

on the lips
for inventing
arepas con queso.
For breakfast,
tía makes the best
ones I've ever had.
She serves them
with fresh cheese
and the creamiest

hot chocolate
known to man.
I'm eating and
watching *Conan*
the Barbarian when
Daniela comes out,
woken up by
the sound of
horses, brutal
axings, and
gladiatorial-style
beatdowns.

What is this? Is this
that Arnold guy?

Schwarzenegger, yes.
He's freaking jacked, right?
Look at his arms.

Marcos, you're weird.
It wasn't enough to watch
bulls commit murder
on the news
before bed,
you gotta watch
people slice
each other in
two while you
eat cheese?

MAN OF THE HOUSE

is what people call me these days.
Aunts, distant cousins, and nosy neighbors

who live to remind me
of my new role as the

only boy in a tribe
of women and girls.

It's extra weight to carry,
and my shoulders feel unprepared.

I protect my sister Daniela
because it's my duty.

And I have no choice but to assume
the role, whether I want to or not.

She starts high school in the fall
and I'm headed to the 11th grade,

meaning we're back to being in the
same school together.

Meaning I have
to be prepared

to square up, catch hands
at the drop of a dime.

Let's just say I know what lies ahead.
I know my stomping grounds

and the fast-talking clowns
who claim it as theirs too.

Utter fools who love to
play tough and kick game

at cute girls, especially freshmen,
they've never met.

But Daniela is strong.
She doesn't budge or bend

whichever way she is told.
Papi raised her to never

let anyone take up space
that is hers and hers alone.

Ma I want to shield
from the sorrow

deep in her soul,
but I can't.

She is busy trying
to shield me from mine.

And when she's not doing that,
she's fluttering around

every which way. Rearranging
bedrooms back home, making trips

to Goodwill, smashing to-do lists.
Putting her energy into things she can control.

But I know it's all a front. A piling on
of activities to try and bury the pain.

ASKED ABOUT MY GRADES IN SCHOOL

I deflect.
Switch the subject.
Bang on the table.
Boom Clat . . . Boom Boom Clat.

Ma slaps my hand.

Tell your tía what you told me . . .

Me: *Huh?*

Ma: *Yeah.*

Me: *What?*

Ma: *What does an F on a math exam stand for?*

Me: *Ma . . .*

Ma: *Tell her.*

Tía: *Tell me.*

Me: *F means Fantastic. Everybody knows that.*

DROPPING CLUES

I drop some lazy, hazy
not-so-subtle hints
about cruising
Cartagena with Camilo.
Random nonsense like:

Have you all seen the movie Taxi Driver *starring Robert De Niro?*

Hey, what did the barber say to the cabbie?

Personally, I love a good yellow car.

Ma says, *I'll think about it, Marcos.*
   Let. Me. Think.

ON MOTHERS AND SISTERS

Even the mother of God could be
overprotective, like a lioness
guarding her cubs.

Sisters can get on your nerves
by barging into your room
unannounced.

But they're all you have
And you're all they've got,
besides those two goldfish
you're pretty sure you forgot to feed.

5 REASONS WHY I LOVE HAVING A SISTER FOLLOWED BY 5 REASONS I DON'T

Love:
1. They understand you more than most
2. They never leave you alone
3. They give you someone to protect
4. They teach you about how girls think
5. They tell you when you're wrong

Don't Love:
1. They understand you more than most
2. They never leave you alone
3. They give you someone to protect
4. They teach you about how girls think
5. They tell you when you're wrong

BACK AND FORTH

Camilo and I have been
exchanging text messages,
trying to figure out
my approach for convincing
my birth-giver he can be trusted.
That I will not end up
in a ditch somewhere.

Camilo, will I end up in
in a ditch somewhere?

His non-reply is concerning
at first. Turns out it's a confusing
American expression which
requires some explanation.

Oh, jajaja. No, Marcos, you will not
end up in a ditch somewhere.

Score? Score.

CERTAIN NAMES

roll off the tongue real
smooth and musical.

Certain names plain sing,
like the person who carries

the name was destined to
be known by the world.

Certain names like
Chaka Khan
Jean-Claude Van Damme
Johnny Cash
Ariana Grande
Gabriel García Márquez

Certain names stick with you,
like loyal friends

or crunchy peanut butter
caked onto the roof of your mouth.

AS FATE WOULD HAVE IT

Ma agreed to set me free.
Or, Camilo helped me break loose
from her shackles,
like in the movie
Shawshank Redemption.
He said, *Put your mom on the phone.*
Camilo then proceeded
to turn on the charm,
assuring Ma I'd be safe
driving around with him
and learning about new things.
Think of it as a field trip, Ma,
I said. *An educational one.*
It helped that Ma and Camilo
found some common ground,
since Ma went to
his junior high and, when he showed up,
the tee he was wearing was from the library
where Papi volunteered as a kid.

So, she gave in, as long as I
promised to check in
every 30 minutes.

Marcos, I need to hear your
voice twice every hour.

Deal.

I'm in the front seat
and Camilo is telling me stories
that remind me of Papi's stories.
Not because of what they're about,
but in the way that he tells them.
Camilo speaks with his hands
and has this contagious laugh.

In between me reading
and him picking up and
dropping off customers,
Camilo talks about Gabo,
which is what they called
Gabriel García Márquez.

CAMILO BREAKS IT DOWN

García Márquez, the son of Gabriel
Eligio García and Luisa Santiaga
Márquez Iguarán, once said this:

All of my books have loose threads
of Cartagena in them.
And, with time, when I have to
call up memories,
I always bring back

an incident from Cartagena,
a place in Cartagena,
a character in Cartagena.

Camilo says:
García Márquez
first arrived in Cartagena
by way of Bogotá
in 1948,
as a young and
hungry writer with empty pockets
and a head full of dreams.
He soaked in local stories
and happenings, later transforming
them into literature that would
cross borders
and make him a star.

When Camilo speaks of
García Márquez
and of their shared Cartagena,
his face lights up like fireworks.
Eyes gleam like the tip
of the cigarette that
dangles from his lips.

They're very much connected,
this writer and this city.
Together as one.
Like one cannot exist
without the other.
García Márquez is Cartagena
and Cartagena is García Márquez.

CAMILO WAS RAISED A LONG WAY

from the cobblestone streets
and magic of the Old Town.
Far from where birds with colorful bills
land on tables to greet happy tourists
enjoying their breakfast.

The slums of Camilo's childhood years,
he says, were filled with such ruthless crime
you wouldn't wish them on your worst enemy.
Where kids with their ribs exposed
set the streets on fire
and desperation ran
as deep as the sea.

Sometimes there wasn't even
running water, Camilo tells me,
and on a few occasions
he saw raw sewage pour out into
parking lots and sidewalks.

Like how in
ONE HUNDRED YEARS OF SOLITUDE
blood and death flow across terraces
and hug walls
and go along porches
and into living rooms
to find who they're looking for.
Of course, Camilo's descriptions make
me want to read more.

I wonder to myself why and how he
seems to bring almost
every conversation we have
back to his favorite novel—
which Ma says was also
Papi's favorite novel—
even when he is talking about himself.
They seem connected, too.

Camilo is

ONE HUNDRED YEARS OF SOLITUDE.

ONE HUNDRED YEARS OF SOLITUDE

is Camilo.

ON TOP OF ALL THIS I WONDER

how many times Camilo
must have read the thing.
It is no small book
or short read.
The copy I hold
in my hand
is 417 pages.
Feels as heavy
as a freaking Bible.

I LOOK OUT THE WINDOW

as we drive,
at the people
and the restaurants
I'm sure Papi would have loved
and the music I know
he would have stopped to move to.

Camilo looks over at me,
sees something in my face,
or maybe sees something else,
and makes a swift U-turn,
pushing me forward in my seat.

We drive
without talking
for a while,
though I now
feel even more
on edge.

I notice Camilo tense up
whenever a police car
goes past us.
It could just be me,
but I doubt it. I know
the look.

PAPI WAS THE SAME WAY

regardless of whether or not
he did anything wrong.
The mere sight of blue and red
was enough to make him uncomfortable.
I never asked him why.

WHAT IS YOUR DREAM?

Papi asked me once.
We were drinking
Slurpees on the curb outside of 7-Eleven.
You mean, besides this?

HONK!

Out of nowhere, Camilo
spots something out of the corner
of his eye and slams on the pedal,
tearing through a stoplight like a lunatic.

We almost clip
the back of a bus
and come within feet of
smashing against a tree.
Next to it stands an arepa vendor,
who, at the speed we were going,

for sure would have been squashed
like a bug. Or maybe we would've spun
over the highway, leaving my sister brotherless

and my mother sonless.

What
The
Hell?

There's a concert of yelling
and honking.
I can feel my pulse
race under my skin.

We turn off the main road
and onto a back street.
The whole thing lasts about 15 seconds,
but feels like a lifetime and a half.
When I ask *What the hell?*
Camilo says he *thought he saw something,*
which may be the worst explanation
in the history of bad explanations.

What am I doing here
and will I survive this?

No, for real.

AFTER DRIVING

for a thousand years
we arrive at
Castillo de San Felipe de Barajas,
which Papi mentioned to me once before.
It's a fortress that was built
in the 1500s and sits on a hilltop
overlooking Cartagena.

Cartagena, the walled city
with a tangled-up history
of fending off invasions
and warring with pirates.
All lured here, I'm told,
on the hunt for riches.

Camilo and I people-watch
some before we set out for
the top of the fortress,
my new friend clutching his book
like a weapon. It's crowded today
and visitors run around snapping pictures
and smiling from ear to ear.
I'm not sure why Camilo brought me here,
but I'm grateful he did.
We gaze out over stretches of land and water
without speaking until . . .

READING ONE HUNDRED YEARS OF SOLITUDE *IS LIKE*

sitting at the highest point
of the highest mountain
and looking down at the people below,
Camilo says.
You watch and study them as they live their lives.
As they bleed from their wounds
write poetry
dream
fall in love
fight in wars
birth sons and daughters
lie and cheat
get eaten by ants
accept their fate.

After you have grown to
love them
or hate them,
they die or disappear
in the wind.
On and on and on.

Camilo pulls out a joint
from his pocket,
sparks it,
and starts up again.

Reading ONE HUNDRED YEARS OF SOLITUDE *is like*
sitting at the highest point
of the highest mountain
and looking down at the people below.
You take a psychedelic mushroom and
watch as they
shoot their leaders
organize uprisings
take new lovers
read ancient manuscripts
exploit workers
alienate themselves from the outside world
wish for better days
accept their fate.

After you have grown to
love them
or hate them,
they get slaughtered and dumped into the sea
or they disappear
in the wind.

It is the story behind every story.

It is the story I take in, finish, and take in again.
Over and over like a revolving door.

Like a love song.

PAPI LISTENED TO LOVE SONGS
LIKE A FIEND

The kind that put raw emotions to words.

The kind about longing and heartbreak and joy.

The kind that make you two-step as soon as they come on.

The kind that feel like a drug.

The kind that made him reach for Ma, kiss her mouth,
and bring her in tight before telling sis and me to please go away.

OUR PARENTS DID

their best to carve out date nights
and such, but overall didn't get much alone
time, except when a friend would volunteer
to watch us here and there. Unlike
most of my friends, we never had grandparents
on standby to look after us.

Not until the last couple of years,
when they trusted their kids
not to murder each other
or burn down the building,
did they dare leave us home alone.

GRANDMOTHERS IN COLOMBIA

are praised
like mini gods.

They're lifted up
and held in
high honor
due to the fact
they have lived
and lived
and lived.

They keep going
and going
and going.

Like the Energizer
Bunny in those
commercials.

They can be superstitious, too.

Camilo says he was brought up
by his grandparents.

In her final years,
his abuela would
preach ad nauseam about
spirits and omens,
signs and wonders.

She spoke of signs
and of things to come.
But always in a serious way.
Always with an unflinching face.

ONE HUNDRED YEARS OF SOLITUDE
is about a woman like this.
The title of the book, Camilo says,
refers to the lonely life of Úrsula,
who lives to be well over one hundred.

She sees, she feels, she suffers.

Imagine the pain and sadness
of outliving everyone
you love and care about.

It was written,

I realize now,
in the style of
Colombian grandmothers.

In how they tell their stories.
With fire.
With heart.

In a way that
sounds supernatural
and borderline unbelievable.
In a way that
surprises you.

In a way that,
because you know
that the person
telling the story
believes in it
more than anything,
you have no choice
but to believe it too.

I know stories like that.

It is not lost on me that Camilo talks about
ONE HUNDRED YEARS OF SOLITUDE
the way Papi talked about Cartagena.

The way a minister
talks about the holy book.
With belief.

Camilo says it has outsold
everything published
in Spanish except
for the Bible.

It is not so different
from the Bible, you know?
The different voices,
the shifting time periods.

I can see what he means.
I wonder why none
of my teachers

ever made us read it
in middle school or even
so far in my high school,
like they do here.

I can't say for sure,
but I have a few guesses.

10 GUESSES WHY NONE OF MY TEACHERS HAVE ASSIGNED *ONE HUNDRED YEARS OF SOLITUDE* TO STUDENTS

1. They think we won't understand it
2. They don't understand it
3. They assume we won't live to be 100 and don't want us to get our hopes up
4. They think it's too many pages for us but that maybe in college we'll be ready
5. They think THE ADVENTURES OF HUCKLEBERRY FINN is more our speed
6. They assign whatever their bosses tell them to assign
7. They don't know us at all
8. They
9. They
10. They

BEING THIS HIGH UP

with Camilo reminds
me of the summer

we went to California.
Papi and his friend took us to
Joshua Tree National Park
to explore and see a side
of Mother Nature
you don't get to
experience in Miami.

Huge boulders.
Desert trees
shaped like slingshots.
Daniela twisted her ankle
climbing up a rugged rock
and Papi had to carry her
all the way down the mountain.
He was always carrying us.

He always   carried us.

GRATEFUL DEAD

Camilo offers me his joint
but I don't take it.
Thanks, but no thanks, parcero,
I say. I hope it doesn't
offend him. That's the
last thing I want to do.

It doesn't seem to bother him.
Thing is, I had some weed once
in 7th grade and the whole ordeal

was mucho dreadful,
thank you very much for asking.

I was at this kid called Miguel's
from two buildings over
when he pulled out his stepdad's bong.
A glass contraption that
resembled something used to conduct
important scientific experiments
with a sticker on it that said
Grateful Dead.
I hit it like Luis showed me
and almost coughed up a lung.
Luis cracked up, obviously.
I cracked up with him.
What an amateur, he said.
After three hits and seven
plays of "I Wanna Get High"
by Cypress Hill, the paranoia
started to settle in.
Everything was spinning.
I was terrified at the thought
of my parents finding out.
Maybe petrified is a better word.
Feels more true.
So yeah, petrified.
Or, petri-fried.
The bike ride home:
What is normally
a 20-second trip
took what felt like
40 days and 40 nights.

I kept riding in circles, disoriented,
unable to find my door,
which, again, is two buildings over.
Two.
Buildings.
Over.
That damn song was stuck
in my head and I kept repeating
the chorus
to myself as I tried
to find where I live.
Eventually I got there
thanks be to God
and I went straight to my bed
and crashed—
        a different kind of crash.

I yank the cancer stick hanging over Camilo's
ear and say, *Now, this I will have.*
I take a puff and immediately it occurs to me
I chose the worse option.

ON THE WAY BACK TO MY TÍA'S HOUSE

gratefulness washes over me
like water cascading
down a mountain.
A sense of gratitude for being
in the motherland.
So far, it's been all
I didn't know I needed.

I wasn't asking for much.
Just wanted to feel *something*.
Brave the streets. Taste the air.
I know it won't last forever.
Until this dream is over,
I'll continue to:

listen to Camilo fire off tales

watch him yell at reckless drivers

read this book I'm glad to have found

write

inhale secondhand smoke

eat my weight in empanadas

try not to think about the new school year

fail at not thinking about the new school year

wonder why Camilo tenses up so bad
whenever a cop rolls by
paying us no mind.

       Is he trying to protect me? If so, from whom?

From what?

He (probably) thinks I don't notice but I do.

And I haven't decided yet if I care enough to ask.
Maybe another time. Maybe never.

WHEN I WALK IN, THERE'S A VISIT IN FULL SWING

Say hello to your cousins, Ma says.
Hugs, hellos, and I'm-sorrys.
Gerardo, who is at least 6'2 and built
like a brick shithouse, takes out $20
from his chain wallet and hands it to me.

Oye, that's from both of us,
his brother Chaco says from
across the room.
These people aren't so bad.
But they're a lot.

An hour or so later, I sneak outside with my book,
the smell of cigarette still on my fingers.
I don't intend to read but the book has become
something like a security blanket.

Thinking:

In just a few short days, I have
seen or met or heard or tasted:
exotic birds (there's over 200 native birds here)
delicious fruits (A man sold us the best papaya ever)
rare flowers (I never once cared about orchids until now)
kind strangers (I have already seen about a thousand smiles)

beautiful sounds (An old woman playing accordion in the street)
lovers on the beach (Can anyone look more in love than people
                    kissing on the sand?)

IT'S A NEW DAY

Of hangs with Camilo
Of ditching Ma, Daniela, and my tía
Of learning more about Gabo

Of exploring the city by taxi
Of pandebonos and buñuelos on Colombian sidewalks
Of falling more in love with the clopping of horse-drawn carriages

Of reading and writing
Of dreaming in another tongue
Of the rest of my life

AT CAMILO'S PLACE—

where he lives with his grandfather
who has Alzheimer's and who on
most days doesn't remember his name—
there are paintings.

Paintings everywhere.

On the walls, the floors,
and leaning against the bookshelves.

Paintings Camilo made himself.
Some have bizarre maps and symbols
that look like mathematical formulas.

One painting, he tells me,
is of his dead brother.
He was finishing it around the time
his brother passed away,
three years ago.
I don't ask how he died.
Camilo says he hasn't forgiven
God for taking him, not yet.

It's a freaky portrait, at least to me.
Maybe disturbing is a better word.
A head and face with three small legs
sticking out of each side like a beetle.
Zippers covering the eyes.
Shaggy hair and bushy lamb chops
like the long-lost twin of John Lennon.

Ah, I get it. A Beatle.

CAMILO ASKS IF I WANT TO PLAY HOOPS

and the question is
beautiful music to my ears.
Does the pope shit in the woods? I say,
but it doesn't translate.
We do a couple more passenger drop-offs
and make our way to a nearby park.

When we pull up in Camilo's taxi
there's a group of kids shooting around
using a soccer ball.
Camilo sighs, opens his trunk,
and grabs his basketball.
My eyes swell up with happiness,
and I think theirs do too.

After intros and handshakes,
we shoot around, warm up, stretch.
A kid about my age asks if we want
to challenge him and his friend
to a game of two-on-two.
Does the pope . . . ?
I stop myself mid-sentence.

IF I HAD TO PICK ONE WORD

to best describe what we do to these boys,
it would be: annihilation.
Complete and utter destruction.
As in, *Excuse me, officer, I would
like to report a murder.*
Me and Camilo look like
Jordan and Pippen.
Lebron and Wade.
Shaq and Kobe.

Trust me, I study the game
and know all the greats
inside and out.

We don't give up a single point—
they don't score once.
I *almost* feel bad.
Camilo's crossover is killer,
his jump shot money in the bank.
My assists are crafty,
and my one-legged fadeaway
keeps falling like dominoes.

There's something about banding together
to ruin someone else's day on the court
that will bring a friendship closer.
It's a bond that starts with sunken threes
and crazy no-look passes.
I can't explain it.
There's a rhythm to it all.
And once it's found, it
is not easily broken.
Did we just become best friends? I say,
quoting Brennan in the movie *Step Brothers*.
That joke lands, thank goodness, and Camilo smiles.

Time to get back to work, he says.
Things get heated between the boys
as we turn to leave. They push and shove
and even throw fists.

As we drive away, one boy is
kicking the other on the asphalt.
I turn to Camilo as if to say
We should go back and help that guy
and he looks back at me with

his lips pursed as if to say
You're only a guest here and that
ain't none of our business, chico.

Two friends scrapping like frenemies,
all for losing bad despite having
home-court advantage.

What a time.
What a time.
What a time.

I can't wait to tell Devon
and Hector about this.

MA SAYS TO BE BACK BEFORE DINNER

She says my tía is preparing
sancocho de pollo, one of Papi's top three meals.

Since Papi died, tía is the only living sibling,
the daughter of two dead parents and the sister
of two dead brothers. Yesterday, she told us
that every now and then she'll cook a hefty meal
and pretend all the siblings are together again.
She always ends up either trashing
pounds of leftovers or bringing them
to the nursing home where she works.
Those two loved to eat, she said,
like kings without a crown.

I ignore Ma's text; although part of me wants to reply,
I'm busy smoking cigs and committing hook-shot homicide,
be back when I'm damn well good and ready.
I'm not here to be Papi's surrogate stomach.

THE TWO VOICES IN MY HEAD

engage in perpetual war.

The Man of the House vs. The Rebel Without a Pause

The Ball Player vs. The Poet

The Mama's Boy vs. The Father's Son

The Gringo vs. The Colombian

The Overachiever vs. The Time-Waster

But who says I can't be all of these things,
and more, at the same time?

Any way you slice the pound cake,

it's always and forever,

forever and always,

Me vs. Me.

A LADY WITH A HAIRNET

rakes leaves outside,
a light drizzle trickling down
her rosy cheeks like tears.

We're sitting outside
on Camilo's steps.
He fires one up.

Tell me a secret, Camilo says,
pulling from his spliff.
I pause for a moment.

What kind of secret? I ask.
Something you've never told anyone,
not even your best friends in the world.

My brain hurts trying
to think of something
as the rain comes down harder.

Camilo puts out
his smoke and motions
toward the door.

But not before pointing at me
as if to say, *Hey, we're not done here.*
Get back to me on that secret.

CAMILO ASKS WHAT I'VE BEEN WRITING

all these days and I tell him *scribbles.*
It's day two or three or seven together,
who knows? We're standing

outside the panadería,
talking smack and throwing
back sodas and cheese bread.

Let's write some haikus, he says.
I shoot him a blank stare.
Don't be an ass. You write three, I write three.

I look down at my busted,
once-white Chuck Taylors which are
stained in grass, muck, and Colombian cola.

It dawns on me:
I've just been challenged
to a haiku battle

outside of a bakery in Cartagena, Colombia
by an 18-year-old high-school dropout
taxi driver who is possibly a genius.

MARCOS

+

Dirty Chucks on feet
battered like this heart of hearts.
I'll go where they lead.

+

Someone with no home
is a someone on the run.
But aren't we all?

+

I do not know why
I can never remember
any of my dreams.

CAMILO

+

I dreamt of oceans
where the waters become tears
that can't be wiped clean.

+

I dreamt aliens
wiped out South America
and no one noticed.

+

I dreamt of Gabo,
again among the living,
at his typewriter.

I CONFESS

I did not know
until this moment
that García Márquez
        Gabo
was not *among the living.*
I don't mention it
to Camilo, of course,
because I feel stupid,
like it's something
I should have known.
Back in the taxi, I do a Google search.
It's true—date of death: April 17, 2014.

The article says:

The Colombian Nobel laureate
Gabriel García Márquez,
who unleashed the worldwide boom
in Spanish-language
literature and magical realism
with his novel One Hundred Years of Solitude,
died at the age of 87. He had been admitted
to a hospital in Mexico City
on 3 April with pneumonia.

How did I miss this?

How did I not pick up on the fact that
García Márquez was dead?

And after Camilo has been rattling
on about him all the livelong day(s)?

Where is he buried? I ask much later,
breaking our silence.

The streets are buzzing
with drifters
and worker bees
going about their business.

Who? Camilo replies,
turning back to me.

García Márquez . . .
where is he buried?

His ashes, Camilo says,
were laid to rest in La Merced.
It's a monastery attached
to the University of Cartagena.

Wait . . . so his ashes are here? I ask.

Yes. After he died in Mexico,
where he had lived for a long time,
his ashes were flown to Cartagena.

His parents are buried here too.
So, they're all together.
Together as a family.

AS FATE WOULD HAVE IT

Papi's ashes will soon be released
in the same city as his idol's.

In the city they both adored,
the city that helped shape them.

Knowing now that García Márquez
is here, I'm convinced this is

what Papi would have wanted.
Though it's also likely that Papi believed

he would live forever young.
I did. I for sure did.

CAMILO READS THE PAPER

as his grandfather sits on his bed
staring at Camilo's beetle painting,
a lifeless look in his eyes.
I lay back on the sofa with my notepad,
jotting down thoughts and underlining passages
in ONE HUNDRED YEARS OF SOLITUDE.
My pen dances on the page like's Papi's hands

prepping steaks in the kitchen.
Or the happy little trees guy with the afro
making everything look easy, on PBS.

Only I'm not making
icy-blue mountains,
log cabins,
and evergreens.

My head
is full of fear
about the future.
But my hands feel   free
between the margins.

I could use a mountain   and a peek
        at whatever is to come.

I hate being this afraid,
but around Camilo
I feel strangely alive.

OUT OF NOWHERE

Camilo starts to talk
about the ashes
of García Márquez.

I've never known anyone
to just start going on about

death and ashes,
but I guess that's Camilo.

And I think I like that about him.
He's got a darkness inside
that feels honest; it's a darkness
I share. From his sense of humor
to his choices of books and songs.

Camilo reaches into his pocket
for a flask and pours
out a few drops of aguardiente.

For Colombia's favorite son,
who is now dust,
Camilo says.

I echo his words —
For Colombia's favorite son.

But I'm thinking of Colombia's
second-favorite son.

FOR ALL OF THE NOVEL'S SUCCESS

and international praise,
one thing García Márquez
never had any interest in was seeing
ONE HUNDRED YEARS OF SOLITUDE
adapted into a movie.

You'd think any author would love the idea
of a film producer bringing their vision to life onscreen.
Plus, García Márquez let studios
make movies and shows
out of other stuff he'd written.
He even dabbled in screenwriting
himself, Camilo tells me.

But ONE HUNDRED YEARS OF SOLITUDE
is another animal. García Márquez decided
not to sell the rights because he believed
it would ruin the magic.

He thought readers around the world
should be free to imagine the characters
how they wanted. To be reminded
of family members, neighbors, friends;
to bring their own lives to the story.
Their own memories.

Letting a filmmaker tie these characters
to specific actors would make the story
something different.
Something, to use Camilo's words,
more narrow, more limited.
It would no longer feel
universal.

Of course, with Gabo gone,
anything is possible. And maybe
there's a way to do it right,
even if it won't be so on his watch.

How sweet it must be, Camilo says,
to be so sure of who you are
and of what you want
and don't want
in this life.
Like Gabo
was.

GABO

I learn, had some
interesting times
as a young writer.

An example is:
for almost a year,
he rented a room
for one peso fifty a night
at a four-story brothel
called The Skyscraper,
in the city of Barranquilla.

His room supposedly
was more like an office cubicle.
Day and night, he wrote and wrote,
toiling away on newspaper pieces
about the small towns
and villages he knew.
Above his room
were the prostitutes' quarters,
where all kinds of
lights, camera, action went down.

Gabo made nice
with the prostitutes
and helped them write letters.
In exchange, they gave him soap
and fed him breakfast.
One of the women,
María Encarnación,
would iron Gabo's
pants and shirts once a week.

At The Skyscraper,
there was noise, violence,
and constant drama
at the worst hours. Much later,
Gabo would say that
even though those were happy days,
he never expected to survive them.

According to Camilo,
those wild nights
were probably great for the writer.

Living through that will
make a storyteller out of you.

MY FATHER TOO WAS

a spinner of tales.
Like Gabo's, Papi's
stories often felt
as old as time itself.

He laced memories
together like a rope chain,
each one its own knot of meaning.

Like the one where
Papi saved a man
from a burning car,
only to find out
that it was
the man's sick brother
who had doused the seats
with lighter fluid and
tossed in the match.

Papi's voice drew
you in like a bassline.
He was pure love
and pure adrenaline
all the time.
Went from 0–100
like that, whether
entertaining friends at our house,
defending the helpless,
or

    riding his motorcycle.

That damn motorcycle!

OTHER THINGS CAMILO KNOWS ABOUT ARE

How to change a tire in five minutes

The first and last names of most of the US presidents

At least six foods that start with the letter Q

The list of US immigration interview questions

How to juggle a Hacky Sack

How to load, cock, and shoot

Why some cats are allergic to humans

Ernest Hemingway's wives

How to perform CPR and the Heimlich maneuver

Driving stick shift

How to keep me guessing

He's super good at that last one.
So much about Camilo
feels like a riddle that'd take
at least 100 Years of Togetherness
to solve. I can only know so much.

I MAY NOT KNOW HALF OF WHAT HE KNOWS

but maybe
Camilo is
who I
would be,
had I
grown up
in Cartagena.
Is this
why I
like being
around him
so much?
Because being
in his
company is
like getting
to understand
an alternate
version of
myself born
in a totally
different world?

PIECES OF A MAN

His generosity,
big old laugh like thunder,
his never-ending curiosity

about how the universe works,
his raised eyebrows
when he's off on a rant,
the way he'll say something
mind-blowingly deep
and then blow smoke rings to lighten the mood,
his never in a hurry,
those beat-up hands that tell you things ain't been easy,
his squeaky-clean cab we lean against to stretch our legs,
the kindness in his tone when he's showing a confused
tourist the way—these things tell
some of the *what* and *who* but could never
express the *whole* that is Camilo.
Like Papi, Camilo is something
to be untangled over time.

WE STOP FOR PIZZA

at a spot Camilo swears by.
I order a pepperoni slice
and a mushroom one.
Camilo gets a plain cheese.
We're starving and don't say much.

The pizza is decent,
even if the theme
of the restaurant is questionable.
Since they cater mostly to travelers,
how it works is
you bring your dirty laundry
and the staff cleans it while you eat.

That's their thing
if you have two hours to spare.
Pay a few bucks and they
serve you grub
and see to your bag
of smelly underwear.

But more unsettling than laundry
as a pizza topping is the way
Camilo's face looks nervous,
once again, when a cop walks in.
Now I've seen him do this
a number of times
and can't shake it.

I see his shoulders tighten
as the man places his order,
a Glock and a long baton
on either side of his waist.

Camilo looks down at his plate
like he's trying not to look up
or meet eyes with the Five-O.
I don't like looking at police either,
but this feels shady.

PLAY IT OFF

I don't
probe

I don't
dig

I don't
question

I will drift down
this cold river
of silence
until the time
is right.

FIVE-SECOND RULE

I drop a chunk of
crust on the taxi floor,
pick it up, and eat.
Camilo responds
with a scowl,
as if he's never heard
of the five-second rule.
Which, it turns out,
he hasn't.

I explain with an
air of supreme confidence
that five seconds
is the precise window
of opportunity
before food dropped
on the floor

is contaminated
or infected
with any harmful germs.
If consumed within that window,
I tell my mesmerized student,
it is safe to eat.
*That is disgusting,
and so are you*, he fires back.

*Marcos, you could not begin
to imagine, not in a billion years,
what repulsive things
have taken place
right there where you sit.
And the floor may be
the most filthy spot of all.
Enjoy your pizza.*

CONFESSIONS

Later on, Camilo
wants to *talk*.
He knows he made
things awkward
in the pizza shop earlier
and says he wants
to explain. He sparks one
up and fixes his posture
like he's in confession.
I remind him I am no priest
and no saint.

He says if we're going
to be pals,
we cannot lie
or withhold important facts
from each other.

It turns out that
up until recently,
Camilo was in a gang.
Colombia, come to find out,
has hundreds of gangs spread
out across all of its major cities.
Kind of like the US.
And in smaller cities like
Bucaramanga, Barranquilla,
and Cartagena,
there are also countless
pissed-off juveniles
who terrorize neighborhoods
and public spaces
without remorse.
Camilo was one of them.
His was in a gang called
Lobos Locos, he says,
but he quit.
Done. Finished.
Came to his senses.
I'm unsure how to respond,
so I don't. Just shut up and listen.

. . . .

. . . .

. . . .

And listen some more.

. . . .

. . . .

. . . .

He sucks his teeth
and keeps talking.

I've done some
horrible things in my 18 years.
Mostly petty crime.
Vandalism.
Graffiti.
Fighting.

Regardless, they are crimes
he's not proud of.

He's leaving the worst parts
to my imagination,
I'm sure, though I'm trying not to judge, or pry.

But something happened
that, according
to Camilo, pushed him to his
breaking point.
Camilo hangs his head,
starts and stops,
starts and stops.
He struggles to speak.
Fiddles with the rabbit's
foot he keeps in his jeans
for good luck.

Finally, it comes out:

Two weeks ago, this idiot Fernando asked
if he could use my taxi to take care
of some business. I was on a break
so I said Yes, thinking nothing of it.
Later that day, he hit someone
with my taxi and fled the scene.
I don't know if the boy he hit is dead
or living, but I learned that he is from a
rival gang, meaning Fernando did it on purpose.

I tried to find out more but discovered nothing, ni mierda.
I wanted to strangle Fernando on the spot,
drain the life from him for putting me in this position.
The next morning, he left for Venezuela,

leaving me to deal with the possible murder weapon.
And a permanent fear that I will somehow,
someday, be punished for something I had
no part in.

But the truth is I am
not completely innocent in all this.
Instead of reporting the crime, Marcos,
I did my best to buff out the dent.
Then I gave the taxi a deep wash
to make sure there was no DNA on its surface
that could implicate me. In the eyes of the law,
these would all be considered acts of an accomplice,
a co-conspirator.

So now I'm always worrying,
What if the cops catch me somehow?
Or what if Fernando decides
he has to come back and finish me off
since I'm the only one who can tie him to the crime?

Anything is possible.

As usual,
I have more questions than answers.

CROSSROADS

With all that
on his back
Camilo had to

leave the life,
sever ties
with old sidekicks,
repent for his sins,
keep to himself,
try to not die,
listen to Gabo,
hope for the best.

He hasn't spoken to
anyone from his old gang
since, he says, they all agreed
to let him be, to *Leave that nerd*
to his reading. Camilo makes it clear
that to be left alone in this way
is a blessing unto itself.
And a rare one.

EVEN IF IT WASN'T HIS FAULT

Camilo's confession triggers
mixed feelings; it makes me think

too closely on how Papi was killed
not to bring me down.

I feel robbed and somewhat lied to.
It makes me question Camilo,

who I have grown
to trust over these last days.

Looking at it from his angle,
I guess I understand.

He didn't know me
well enough to immediately

spill his guts. He doesn't
owe me anything.

But now we're boys.
Why can't anything be easy?

I SEARCH AND SEARCH

But instead of seeing anything
about a hit and run, I find a depressing
article about a 13-year-old Cartagena
boy who died of kidney failure
after years of sniffing glue.

Glue?
Glue.

Santiago had been living alone
near Calle Media Luna
after his parents
abandoned him at age ten.
With no way of forking over
the $50,000 for a kidney transplant
that could have spared
his life, Santiago died. Dead.

How can anyone let this
happen? I ask.

Camilo fills me in
on the street urchins
who sniff
industrial-
grade glue
around Sector La Magdalena
and El Paraiso.
He's seen them before.
The down-and-out youth
who inhale toxic
fumes to get high,
forget about their pain,
and kill their hunger.

Camilo says they
get it from sketchy
markets and street pharmacists.

They keep it in small bottles
or Ziploc bags.
It feels like rubber cement,
Camilo says, it's
amber-colored and sticky.
The boys roam about
looking half-dead.
Looking for their next hit.
Or hunting for an exit.

Maybe they want to die,
because maybe death
is better than hunger.

IT'S BEEN OVER TWO WEEKS

since the accident.
The accident that was
no accident at all.
I search on my phone again
for any news piece that could
back up what Camilo has told me,
or anything that might give us
information about the victim.

Is he dead?
Paralyzed for life?
Still nothing.

The only evidence I have,
if you can call it that,
is Camilo's confession.
and the small dent
on the front bumper
of his taxi.

I DECIDE IT MIGHT BE BEST

to get some space from Camilo,
at least for a couple of days, maybe more.

I don't text back. Don't pick up.
I help my tía around the house,
fold laundry, play checkers with
Daniela. Ma can tell
something is bothering me
and assumes it's just good
old-fashioned sadness
over Papi. And it is, and maybe
always will be. But it's also
a mountain more.

I've come to trust Camilo.
I've come to believe everything
he says and accept it as truth.
I don't want our friendship
to be frayed and stained
like a hand-me-down sweater.
But I also don't want
to be dragged into danger,
especially as this trip starts
to wind down. Papi would tell
me to guard my heart and stash the key
in a vault with a complicated password.
He'd tell me to use my head.

Ma wraps her arms around me and
wells up. My tears don't want to fall.
But if they do, I'm sure she'll try
to catch every last one.
Today . . . mostly sucked.

SECOND AND THIRD THOUGHTS

Two months or so ago
I would have told you
I knew it all.

Up from down,
left from right,
in and out.

But disaster has
a way of seeing
to it that your

questions outnumber
your answers.
You second-

and third-guess
everything like
it's going

out
of
style.

MEMENTOS / MOMENTOS

Tía pulls out
a shoebox stuffed with pictures
of siblings and friends.

The girls giddy
in their too-short shorts
and floral bikini tops

and the boys in swim briefs,
bare-chested,
and grinning.

None of them
looked as if they
might die young.

But don't we all,
even in the smallest ways,
brush shoulders

with death,
daily, hourly,
every minute?

THIS CITY, IN THE 1990s,

might have been
described as a utopia,
depending on who you asked.
People might talk about the parties
and the best moments of their youth.
Maybe, like my tía, they would
tell you about their long walks
and weekends spent
with relatives in the north,
surrounded by
sky-high palm trees
and cloud forests.
Half of her stories
seem to end
with Papi and my tío
grilling whoever looked
at their sister sideways.
I know what that's like.
Tía makes the sign of the cross.
Those boys, she says,
taking a sip of her tea.
Dios los bendiga.
They completed me.

Ma excuses herself.

ROAD RAGE

Tía needs to make
a run to the store
and I volunteer to go with.
Her car has two flat tires
until tomorrow so
she calls for a taxi.
Up rolls a chill guy with
thick-rimmed glasses.

Halfway into a bad
Bruce Springsteen chorus,
we're cut off by a man
in a run-down pickup;
he pulls ahead as
we approach a light,
catching our peaceful
driver by surprise.

Tía leaps out and rushes
straight to the man's
window. She curses
and has a fit.

I panic and go
to try and calm her,
shaking in my shoes.
What if the man has a gun?
A bat?
A giant sword like Conan?

Will he let this slide?
The man stares back,
but doesn't react. His
black eyes barely move.

After she's yelled
every insult she can think of,
we turn around, but our taxi is

    gone

        baby

            gone.

Camilo, truth be told,
never would have left us.
We walk the
last three blocks
to the market
named Macondo,
grab a few things,
and enjoy a drama-free
return home. A lump
sits in my throat
the size
of a small fist.
The woman is just
like her brother(s).

BAPTIZED BY VIOLENCE

In their day, Papi
and my tío dished out
beatings like get-well-soon cards.

Skilled and devastating
beatings, I've been told.
They were brawlers

through and through,
taught by their mother
young to never back down

if pushed to the water's edge.
To strike first, but
only if provoked.

Only if there
was no other solution
than to throw hands.

Papi said
the only defense
against bad people

who commit violence,
is good people
who are better at it.

Tío later became a local boxing champion.
Papi found the love of his life,
his knuckles washed clean.

BACK IN THE DAY

we'd watch pro wrestling.
The classics mostly.
The girls would go for ice cream
or to get their nails pretty
and Papi would bust out
WWE tapes that he
loved from way back.

Our favorite
was Razor Ramon.
The slick-haired heel
who donned purple-
and-yellow trunks
and a neck full
of gold chains
that swayed across
his muscled chest
like a pendulum.
The ultimate bad guy
who flicked toothpicks
at foes and shot
a cocky smirk.
The Razor who talked
a good game
and backed it up.

Papi and me
in front of the tube
launching pillows
and high-fives
into the air
as our main man
laid down the law
and we rooted for the villain.

Say hello . . . to the Bad Guy!

I AM THINKING

about the boy
who was smashed
by Camilo's taxi.
I am wondering
if he's alive.
I am betting
that he's handicapped.
From the waist up, or
from the waist down.
I am building
nightmares in broad daylight.

I am asking myself
what he may
or may not
have done to
deserve to be
black-and-blued

by a good-for-nothing
loser like Camilo's
former friend,
and now enemy.

Our enemy.

ON THE TOPIC OF ENEMIES

I've only been in one fist fight.
It was quick and it was harebrained.
Fast but not furious.
It was in 7th grade,
in Mrs. Shore's Home Economics class.
We were making baked mac and cheese.
This tool Adrian thought I was
through with the stove.
I wasn't through with the stove.
He pushed me
and spat something slick
under his stank breath.
I pushed him back,
not in the mood.
He cracked me in the head.
Nothing I couldn't handle.
I returned the favor
and socked his metal mouth.
Not our most damaging punches.
We shoved. We said words.
As we went to reengage, Mrs. Shore
jumped in and got binked

with an accidental elbow.
A casualty of war.
That was my only fight.
I was suspended for two days.
And on the third day I rose again.

WHEN THEY WERE CHILDREN

tía says their father
blasted tango music
big-time, loved
the tenderness and drama
of pianos, flutes, and violins
melding together.
He hummed "La Cumparsita"
out and about in public
and around the house.

"La Cumparsita"
was written in the 1900s
by a teenage boy
called Gerardo Matos Rodriguez.
Originally, the song had no words, tía says.

I'm only half-listening now.
I glance at my book
dog-eared on the counter,
wishing it closer
as if the Force was with me.
You know that nagging feeling
of putting something you'd

rather be doing
on hold.

Outside the window,
two men argue over
a parking space,
like they're fighting for
the chance to be heard or

felt.

Tía says a version
of La Cumparsita
was later produced with
accompanying words.

It began: *The parade of
endless miseries marches
around that sick being
who will soon die of grief.*

The situation escalates
  outside
and one of the men
swings a knife or stick
and the people scatter.
We don't look up or out
as it all unfolds,
choosing to focus
  inside
on our own

problems—
instead of a stranger's.

IN HIS TEEN YEARS

my grandfather
was a painter.
A prodigy, I'm told.
He was caring
and openhearted,
hungry for the world
and all it had to give.

What kind of painter?
I ask my tía.
She points to a piece
above the sofa
of a man hunched
forward in a chair.
Serious eyes,
broad strokes of
blues, greens, and reds.

At sixteen, my grandfather
would invite randoms into
his parents' home
to do their portraits.
Beggars.
Day laborers.
He'd save cash from
his small allowance

and, when he'd saved what
he thought was enough,
offer men on the street
a few bucks in exchange
for using them as models.

Some of the paintings
were of single figures,
others showed two
or three men
standing or sitting
elbow to elbow.
He captured their
body language
and facial expressions
with, to use my tía's words,
the *generosity*
of an artist twice his age.

At eighteen, he met
my grandmother,
and soon she got pregnant.

One baby, then two, then three.
It wasn't long before
he had to abandon his passion
and provide, because
dreams don't keep the lights on.
He never forgave
the world for making him
bury his gift

in the dirt.
A time capsule
never to be dug up again.

SOME THINGS ARE NEVER MEANT

to be buried.

Dreams.
Talent.
Birthday wishes.

Raw meat near your tent.
A sink full of dishes.
Dead pets in the garden.

Sidebar: Is it worse for a child
to bury their parent or a parent
to bury their child?

POINT OF FACT

Burial has

      forever changed and altered our everyday.

It has taken our—

            stripped our—

                                                    denied our—

chance to be fully—

                        totally—

                                            entirely—

our.

In *our* story, there is a

death and a burial, but no resurrection

                        at the top of the (h)our.

THE GRAND ESCAPE

Once, Papi told us about a night
when he was eleven years old
and planned to run away.
He'd thought about it for weeks.
After careful consideration,
he decided to do an experiment instead:
to see how long it would take for anyone
to notice he was gone.
Papi walked across the street
and knelt in some bushes.
He waited patiently under the silver moon,
holding a small flashlight.
An hour passed, and then two.

Nothing.
No shoes, Papi crouched on all fours on a bed
of dying flowers. His eyes fixed on the apartment.
His brother and sister sat beside the radio
in their pajamas. Where he may or may not
be was the furthest thing from their minds.
His parents argued in the next room.
Fed up, his father eventually left and got into
their old Volvo. He sat there alone. Thinking. Plotting.
The car was raggedy, the paint chipping at every inch.
After about ten minutes, his father turned the key,
but the car did not start. A few more attempts
and the engine came alive.
His mother sat in the kitchen
alone with a cup of coffee.
She cried softly,
so the kids wouldn't hear.

Until that moment, the idea of leaving like that
had always carried appeal for Papi.
The thought of some grand escape
had sparked a thrill inside him.
In primary school, he told us, his favorite stories
were the ones where the main character shoved off
someplace in search of knowledge or treasure.

This fantasy must have run in the family.
Hiding in the dirt, that was the last time
Papi ever saw his father.

HARD TO FIND

A good man
A good cry
A good popsicle joke
A good photo of Bigfoot
A good sequel
A good prequel
A good excuse
A good pair of sandals
A good sparring partner
A good shot of a UFO
A good pops

WHAT IS YOUR DREAM? (#2)

I ask myself.
To someday be the father
Papi was to me,
that his father never was to him.

WHEN I WAS FIVE

I got lost
during a visit
to the museum.

It all started
out peacefully, perfectly.

The four of us
walking around
seeing the exhibits.
We were all playing together
in the germ-infested
pretend grocery store,
when I wandered off
to check out Pirate Island.

All it took
was two seconds
to break free.
Two unattended seconds.

According to Ma,
when Papi and
Ma turned and
realized that I
had gone missing,
they panicked.

I guess Papi
thought *Ma* was
watching me. She
thought that *he*
was watching me.

Following his instincts,
Papi bolted toward
the main entrance,
worried he'd see
someone peeling out

with me in
a white van.
Like in the movies.

But Daniela spotted me
just ten yards away.
Decked out in
a pirate's hat
and eye patch,
swinging a hook.

She didn't know
anything was happening.
From her stroller,
she pointed and
yelled, laughing, like
she always did.
Marcos! Marcos! Marcos!

She got Ma's attention,
who swooped in
and grabbed me.
Papi came back
to see me
safe and smiling
in Ma's arms.

They let out
a deep breath
and Ma gave a
heated speech
about staying together.

About never drifting.

Then we continued
with our fun,
hand in hand.

But to me,
for a minute,
home was a
pirate ship.
Jack Sparrow
cosplay at
the children's
museum.

I never knew
I was lost.

MA GREW UP CATHOLIC

and when we were small,
she would pray
with us before sleep.

On the nights she was
on the phone
or busy with housework,

she had Papi put us
to bed and would ask
him to pray with us.

He never did.
Instead, he read poetry
to us. Poems about politics,

war, and freedom of expression.
I remember a long one
about how the best minds of the writer's
generation were torn apart by madness,
starving and butt booty naked.
The topics in the poems

Papi smuggled into our room
like drugs were rarely comforting,
and probably not age-appropriate.

But the poems always made us think.
The words made us consider things
that had never before crossed our minds.

They stretched our brains
like Laffy Taffy.
And we loved it.

One of our best secrets was
Papi's mastermind deception.
Poetry disguised as prayer.

I'M TEN YEARS OLD

and the actor John Leguizamo
is yelling on the TV.

He's starring in his
one-man stage play
called *Spic-O-Rama*.
In the show,
Leguizamo portrays
all six characters
of a nutty family
in New York City.
The opening skit introduces us
to a boy they call Miggy,
who remembers the time
he was called a stupid, ugly *spic*
by a mean kid at summer camp.
I could have beat him up
so bad, Miggy says.
When you're angry, oh, my God,
you could just beat up people who are a million
zillion trillion times your size.
Through his braces,
Miggy tells me, and Papi,
about how he turned it all around
using Jedi mind tricks.
Yes, yes, yes, I am a spic.
I'm . . . I'm spictacular.
I'm . . . I'm spictorious.
I'm . . . indespicable.

The point?
Maybe words are weapons.
As mighty as fists from someone
who knows how to use them.

MY PARENTS ALWAYS TAUGHT ME

to never go looking for a fight.
But if a problem swung my way,

I had permission to respond or retaliate.
Even though those types

of problems almost never came,
I appreciated the sentiment.

Papi told me there's a major
difference between being kind

and being a doormat.
Be courteous, show respect: Always.
Be soft, let people walk over you: Never.

You are a Cadena, Papi would say.
You are your father's son
and your uncle's nephew.

But you can be like Miggy
when you need to.
Smart with your words.

PAPI DREAMT

of putting a finger
over the world's grief.

Placing his thumb
over its aching parts
to stop
or slow
the bleeding.

Tía says this,
holding back
Niagara Falls
from her eyes.
Her lower lip quivers,
slightly.
She is somewhere else.
Clearly.

I SIT ALONE

thinking about heaven and hell.
Not because I thought of it on my own.
There's a pamphlet on a stack of mail
that says *¿Crees en el cielo y el infierno?*

Do you believe in heaven and hell?

If I'm being real, I've never
thought about it much.
My guess is most kids my age
live day by day according
to this life and worry less
about life in another dimension.

But if I had to answer the question now,
at this moment, I would say,
Yes, si, creo en el cielo y en el infierno.

But are they physical spaces,
under or above the earth's surface?
Are they metaphorical inventions?
Or are they places you go to in your mind
to help describe the indescribable?

HEAVEN ON EARTH

A perfect swish
The right lyric at the right time
Every sip of a cold Mexican coke
The embrace of your birth-giver
The first swim of the year around March

HELL ON EARTH

The death of a hero
Stage 5 cancer
Mrs. Rubin's third period Algebra
Disease and famine
Natural disasters wiping out thousands

Heaven and hell: beautiful and terrible and dangerous.

WHAT IS YOUR DREAM? (#3)

I whisper to my grandfather who's lying
in his grave. *To paint the world as it is,*
he says. *But the right colors keep slipping
through my hands.*

PAPI STARES BACK AT ME

in the bathroom mirror.
On my face, he is still very much alive.
My chocolate eyes are his.
The tip of my nose, his.
My mouth and jaw have the same curve as his.
My brown, unruly head of hair, his.

If my mustache ever grows in thick.
If my shoulders ever get broader.
If I ever hit the growth spurt I've been promised
I will by my old gym teacher,
people who knew Papi will look at me
and not know what to make
of this fishy witchcraft
that makes the dead alive again.

LATELY I'VE BEEN THINKING

about inheritances.
A long word for the gifts and curses
passed down from our bloodline.

Not just physical traits but also
personality quirks, the stuff
sprinkled into the fiber of our DNA.

Papi gave me his
stubbornness, clean heart,
and diehard distrust of authority.

Ma blessed me with her unbendable will,
her tendency to overthink,
and soft spot for other people's pain.

Take any of this away and I feel
incomplete. A ham with no burger.
Chips Ahoy! with no milk.

UNRELATED TO THAT, I'M AT A LOSS

I don't think I'm equipped to organize
the right letters that form the right words
to make the right sentences to
express exactly how I feel about

where I am in my reading,
so I'll put it this way:

This book is
    something *else*.

MIDAFTERNOON MUSINGS ABOUT MACONDO

Let's go to Macondo!
   Where it's scorched, suffocating, chaos
   Where the Buendías traveled through
   mountains and swamps on a worthless
   quest for a promised land

Let's go to Macondo!
   Where banana workers were taken out
   by their own government
   Where nothing is more true than the sea

Let's go to Macondo!
   Where goons wield machetes
   like they're toothpicks
   Where Gabo look-alikes sip
   cervezas at shady bars
   and swap tales with bums
   hovering over the glow of jukeboxes

Let's go to Macondo!
   Where yellow butterflies appear as
   symbols of love
   Where the ordinary meets the impossible

Let's go to Macondo!
   Where the streets are flooded with lies and liars,
   children at play, and language
   Where the people band together against tyrants

Let's go to Macondo!
  Where the wealthy
  rub elbows with the poor
  Where anything and everything
  can turn into nothing in an instant.

I'M THINKING OF THE PART OF THE NOVEL

where Father Nicanor Reyna, the priest
of the town of Macondo,
sets out to prove the existence of God.

Everyone in the town watches as he
drinks from a cup of steaming chocolate,
shuts his eyes, and levitates
almost a foot off the ground.

The only person who doubts
the authenticity of this display
is José Arcadio Buendía,
the highest-ranking man
of the Buendía family and founder
of the town of Macondo itself.

I don't want to give away too much
but I adore how García Márquez
breaks down Buendía
and his doubts,
and how even the priest stops
trying to convince Buendía of anything,
questioning his own faith in the process.

I don't know if Papi believed in God,
but this section reads like a story
Papi would have told us
before bed
    when we were supposed to be praying.

CALLING ALL SPIRITS

I welcome whatever spirit possessed García Márquez
so that he could write like someone not of this planet.
I'm more than halfway through the novel and I keep going back
to reread other sections that I remember as I get further along
in the book. Early in the story, José Arcadio Buendía
wants to leave Macondo with his wife Úrsula and their young son.
She refuses.

Úrsula reminds her husband
that Macondo is the birthplace of their son, and for
this reason alone, they are bound to it, maybe forever. Buendía
tells her that a person doesn't belong to a place until someone is
six feet in the ground. I know this book is not about me, OK?
But lines like this make me wonder where *I* belong.
Is home a person or is it a place?

MUCH LATER, ÚRSULA WORRIES

that her son Colonel Aureliano Buendía,

like his father before him, spends too much time in the lab.

She says:

Children inherit their parents' madness.

I read the words over and over again,

rearranging them in my mind.

Their parents; madness inherit children

Parents / inherit / children / madness / their

Children / mad / their / parents / inherit

Inherit / children / parents / their / madness

I MUST ADMIT

Spending time with this book
in Cartagena has been sweet.
Reading it already felt like magic.

But reading it *here*,
in the city where Gabo haunts every street,

and now,
during the cloudiest
months of my life,

is another kind of special.
It's become more to me than just

My Father's Favorite Book,
or, as Camilo calls it,
The Story Behind The Story.

It makes me feel
as if anything is possible.

There is heaven and hell
and everything in between
    the lines.

I glance at the bookmark
Camilo gave me, which has a quote
from Gabo's speech after he won
the Nobel Prize for Literature, in 1982:

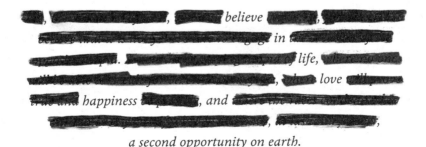

a second opportunity on earth.

Gabriel García Márquez

I REALIZE WHAT I NEED TO DO

is see Camilo.
Patch things up.
Get over it.
Nobody's perfect,
and I miss that joker.
I shoot him a text:
come pick me up.
I grab my backpack
and book, bookmark and all.
Some hours pass
and Camilo's cab is outside.
And just like that,
we're gone
with the quickness.
What can I say?
I guess second chances
(giving them, getting them)
run in the family.

WATCHING THE WORLD PASS BY

through the window of Camilo's cab
makes me feel sad and joyful
all at once.

The constant changes   of scenery
The rotating cast   of characters
How what you see outside   can affect what takes place inside.

Does that make sense? Has this ever happened
to you? Even life's whatever moments
can seem romantic when seen
from the other side of laminated glass.

I have decided that Colombia,
Cartagena to be exact,
is the most amazing place
in existence. You might say,
But Marcos, how can you possibly know that
when you haven't been anywhere,
when you've hardly traveled?
Have you seen Machu Picchu in Peru?

Table Mountain in Cape Town, South Africa?
How about the River Seine in Paris?
Have you been there?

To all of that I say, *No, but trust me.*
Does this look like a face that would lie?

THE CARTAGENA SUN

paints me like my ancestors.
Paints me like Papi's stories
and off-the-wall memories,
which have left
permanent marks on me
like tattoos on the mind.

Colombia is more than the
birthplace of Shakira's hips
that don't lie
and the empires of evil
that once called the shots.

I see why Papi
was so protective
of how others
viewed his country.
He wanted me,
and everyone else,
to understand it is
more beautiful

and complicated
than peoples'
closed-minded ideas.

All I see today
are birds of peace
and not war.

Love and not bullets.

SO FAR IN MY TIME HERE

I have shed pieces of myself
around the city. Before I go,

I hope to leave more
parts of me behind.

I want to learn to accept
things as they are.

To stop worshiping the past,
so that I can live again.

Papi is done living,
and I can only hope I am not done shedding.

CAMILO COMPLIMENTS MY SNEAKERS

and I say, *Thank you, they're Air Jordan 1s.*

He says, *I know, very classic.*

I say, *Yes, maybe the most clutch basketball shoe ever.*

He says, *The ones Michael wore when he scored 63 points in
        the 1986 playoffs.*

I say, *Yessir, and look at you, in your Karl Malones.*

He says, *Thank you, they're worn out but super comfortable.*

I say, *We annihilated those punks the other day.*

He says, *Annihilated?*

I say, *Yes, demolished, defeated, and damn near executed in
        broad daylight.*

He says, *We're like the 1992 Olympic Dream Team.*

I say, *Sure, a man can dream.*

He says, *Dream on, dreamer.*

I say, *I forgive you for not telling me about the accident sooner.*

He doesn't say anything, but also says it all.

ODE TO THE DREAM TEAM

First, the starting five:

Michael Jordan, who launched
into the *Air* and stole its name.

Earvin Johnson, crowned *Magic*
because of his wizardry.

Charles Barkley, who was called a host of things
but mostly *Sir Charles,* as his skills
on the hardwood demanded respect.

Karl Malone, an offensive weapon
whose poise and power always delivered,
earning him the title of *The Mailman.*

Patrick Ewing, who rocked a high-top fade
and remains one of the craftiest shooting centers
the game has seen.

They were style.
They were grace.
They were one.

They also had . . .

Larry Bird: buzzer beater, nasty passer,
king of getting in your head

David Robinson: post-up god, six-time All-Star,
two-time NBA champ

John Stockton: pure point-guard,
shoot it, dish it, steal your ball

Christian Laettner: college highlight reel,
handsome devil, steal your girl

Scottie Pippen: killer handles, A-1 defender, strong as a bear

Chris Mullin: left-handed bucket sinker,
flat-top-having white boy, handles for days

Clyde Drexler: labeled Clyde *The Glide* for a reason

The 1992 Olympic Dream Team.

They were style.
They were grace.
They were one.

CAMILO'S GRANDPARENTS

took him and his brother in
after their parents died.
His grandmother, Camilo says,
as we lounge around in the house
where they raised him,
would never have let him
loan that taxi to anyone.

She was wise, he says.
She understood that people
have their own motivations.

Humans are selfish.

For some reason,
Camilo didn't hear his
grandmother's voice guiding
his moves that day,
like he sometimes does.
I say that I sometimes hear Ma's
voice in my head, too.
It's a whisper or warning
that I ignore
and then regret ignoring later.
I always promise myself that
I will listen
to her the next time.
But you know how that goes.

ACCORDING TO CAMILO, WE'RE ALL RUNNING

from something,
or someone.
And that includes
running from ourselves.
He rubs the right
side of his face,
massages his stubble.

Every person
who is alive
is on the run.
We run from
life and death,
problems and solutions,
questions and answers.

We go back and forth
between leaving and staying,
friends and enemies.

We are always moving,
always running, always
second-guessing.

I have never met anyone
like Camilo.
Listening to him
is like getting
drunk in a maze.

Still . . .

I GET THE FEELING

that when Camilo sounds off
saying *we* and *us* and *our,*
he is talking about himself.
It seems impossible for anyone
to know all of what everyone thinks.

A lot of what he says
sits well with me, maybe 89 percent.
The other 11 percent flies
over my head
like a rocket leaving orbit.

Maybe he attaches
we and *us* and *our* to
his statements and theories
to feel less alone.

Loneliness might be
the worst epidemic
in the world,
if you ask me.
I think José Arcadio Buendía
would agree.
iykyk.

CAMILO NOTICES

I've been eating
through the pages
like an apex predator
and advises me to
please
slow
down.
To savor each
word and sentence,
paragraph and page.

I tell him
that I am.
I say don't tell
me how to eat.

This book is:

Letters stacked
on top of each
other like blueberry
pancakes. Words
flipped and scrambled
like morning eggs
drizzled with hot sauce.
Lines strung together
like home fries
and diced ham.
Each paragraph
flowing into
the next
like chicken
and waffles.
Whole pages
made to guzzle
up like leftover
milk after a giant
bowl of Cinnamon
Toast Crunch.

As Ma used to say
to Papi: My compliments
to the chef.

IT'S SUNDAY AND CAMILO

invites me to attend mass with him.
Ma says it's OK.
In a matter of days, we'll be releasing
Papi's ashes, and I tell her
I want to say some prayers.

There's a small church Camilo
visits from time to time.
You might like it, he says.

I haven't been to church
since the funeral.
And before that, who knows?
Camilo says it helps him
be more aware of his existence
and remember what is important.

I don't tell him that, for me,
church is a symbol of death
and dying. How do you
tell someone that what gives them life
reminds you of the day
death came knocking?

AT CHURCH I SEE

Glass windows.

Oranges, blues, and greens.

Believers and nonbelievers on bended knees.

AT CHURCH I SEE

Candles everywhere.

Shepherds, wise men, and angels.

Paying homage to baby G-O-D.

AT CHURCH I SEE

An image of Christ.

Holding seven stars in his hand.

Prayers, singers, and counters of sheep.

BACK AT HIS HOUSE, CAMILO

coughs
up
some

blood
in
the
bathroom
sink
like
it's
no
big
thing.

But
I
know
something
is
up
if
someone
coughs
up
blood.

LAST NIGHT, GARCÍA MÁRQUEZ

visited Camilo in a series of dreams.

As he drives me back to Tía's, Camilo says:

The dreams felt as real

and smelled as real

and looked as real

as you do sitting

right here, right there

next to me, Marcos.

CAMILO TRIES TO DESCRIBE HIS DREAMS

which sound like
hallucinations or
Choose Your Own Adventure stories.

My arms are crossed and my ears ready
to give him a chance.

I wonder if Camilo has become so obsessed
with García Márquez that the author is
infiltrating his subconscious,

taking on different forms and faces,
the good, the bad, the ugly.
He tries again . . .

LIVING THE DREAM

Last night,
the greatest writer

who ever lived came to me
in a dream and saved me from bleeding
to death from stab wounds I suffered in a fight.
I was looking for my mother in an alley but instead
found a man with a knife. I was on the street dying when
a stranger saw me and rushed me to the emergency room.
The doctor who treated me was none other than the king of kings
Gabriel García Márquez.

Last night,
the greatest writer
who ever lived came to me
in a dream. I was lying on the cold street
on the brink of death and bloody murder when
a Good Samaritan picked me up, carried me into
his truck, and rushed me to the hospital. When we arrived,
I opened my eyes to see that this perfect stranger
who saved me from the pit of hell was our man
Gabriel García Márquez.

Last night,
the greatest writer
who ever lived came to me
in a dream. As I searched for my
mother in the dark and moody streets
of our beloved Cartagena, a man approached
me and asked if I remembered him, which I did not.
He mumbled some things I did not understand and then
pulled out a shiny blade. The man cut me three times
and stood over me whispering The Lord's Prayer. I fixed
my eyes on his and saw that it was the greatest killer who ever wrote
Gabriel García Márquez.

I DON'T KNOW

what to make of Camilo's dream(s).
I'm not positive if he's looking for me
to help decode them or he's just
satisfied with me listening.
Hearing.
Not judging.
All I know is Sundays are supposed to be for rest,
and I am no therapist or interpreter of dreams.

I'VE BEEN HERE

however many days now
and Camilo's taxi has become
a part of my body.

It's where I:
eat
drink
dream
write
doubt
break wind
lie about breaking wind
watch
look.

It's where I listen to Camilo describe his
confusing episodes

and share cloudy visions
that sound like low-budget
movie plots. Each day together
feels like an escape.

I HAVE NO IDEA

I say to Camilo when he asks
me what I make of his dreams.
His dreams about the famous author
who is evidently also his:

doctor
helper
killer

I HAVE NO IDEA

I repeat when he asks me again.
But if I had to pull something
out of my butt for you I would say

hmm let me think . . .

maybe
the dream is about
how the ones
we care about the deepest
and the people we hold up the highest
are the same ones

who in the end
break our hearts.

THEN

Camilo says
with a straight face
I bet your Papi
who helped you
with your nightmares
could have helped me
figure out the meaning
of my dreams.

Yeah,   no   duh.

No   duh,   yeah.

ARE YOU HUNGRY?

seems like a simple question
for another Monday afternoon
shooting the shit at Camilo's.
Yes or *no* seem like simple answers.
But when you're hungry for so much—
food, stories, new ways to feel
about old things—
the question is that much more
sticky/tricky/touchy.
I'm always hungry,

but instead of just saying that,
I say: *Why are the women*
in Gabo's novel always named
Úrsula, Amaranta, and Remedios?

And why is every man in this family
so hungry for power?

Dammit, Camilo says, *do you want*
some lunch, yes or no?

This book is messing
with my head.

CAMILO SHOWS ME A PHOTO

of García Márquez and I remember
where I've seen it before.
Papi had the same photo
of the author, cut out from a newspaper
article. It was on his desk
next to a stack of magazines.
In the photo, García Márquez
sports a black eye.
Like he's been punched.
Don't know why.
I don't ask but
think to myself.
Was he a fighter too?
Like the Cadenas?
They had the same mustache,

Papi and García Márquez.
Thick.
Dark.
Friendly.
A mustache of mustaches.
King level.
Someday I'll have one too.

HOW DOES THIS END?

Does Camilo have a plan?
He can't run forever.
OK, he's not necessarily on the run,
and he doesn't know for sure
if anyone is trying to find
him. But if that boy turns up dead,
does that make Camilo,
who is technically responsible for the taxi,
an accessory to murder?
Can he prove he is innocent
if the law comes asking?

MANTRA

Don't tell Ma
aM llet t'noD

Don't tell Ma
aM llet t'noD

Don't tell Ma
aM llet t'noD

Don't tell Ma
aM llet t'noD

Don't tell Ma
aM llet t'noD

Don't tell Ma
aM llet t'noD

Don't tell Ma
aM llet t'noD

Don't tell Ma
aM llet t'noD

Don't tell Ma
aM llet t'noD

Don't tell Ma
aM llet t'noD

Don't tell Ma
aM llet t'noD

Don't tell Ma
aM llet t'noD

Don't tell Ma
aM llet t'noD

Don't tell Ma
aM llet t'noD

Don't tell Ma
aM llet t'noD

Don't tell Ma
aM llet t'noD

That's 1 *Don't tell Ma* for every year I've lived on this earth.

And 1 *Don't tell Ma* in reverse for every year I've been living
    backwards.

SEMI-SPOILER ALERT

José Arcadio Buendía
lives part of his final years
tied to a chestnut tree.
After he's brought inside,
his wife Úrsula
feeds and cares for him.
Buendía consoles himself
with dreams of freedom.

When Buendía dies
mysteriously—
by murder or suicide
or neither of those—
there's a for real, for real
shift in the wind.

Even nature mourns
the man's death.
Outside the window,
the people see
a light rain of tiny
yellow flowers falling.

But his ghost lives on,
visiting his wife
and roaming the town.

I set down the book
and wonder: has Ma
ever seen the ghost
of the only man
she ever slept with?

CAMILO DECIDES WE DO WANT LUNCH

He wants to go alone
to grab us some food.
Since I've known him
he's paid for everything,
using the tips he earns from
our rides to get the goods.
I've tried to chip in—
for drinks and savory treats
from the bakery—but he
always insists on paying:

In Colombia, generosity is our spiritual gift.

This time I don't give up,
and hand him $17,
which he finally accepts.

No reading Gabo while I'm out,
he shouts over his shoulder.
Watch some television for once.

Then he heads to the door,
crumples and throws the cash
I gave him back on his kitchen table,
and runs out laughing.

Generosity strikes again.

COLOMBIAN SOAP OPERAS HAVE IT ALL

Big boobs and butts.

Tears, tragedies, tantrums.

Anger, action, arson.

I used to watch these telenovelas
with Ma when I was tiny.
Back when Papi worked
as a doorman on Collins Avenue.

Sometimes he had to go to bed early,
so me and Ma would stay up
getting wrapped up in the crazy
lives of these characters on TV.

Ma oohing and aahing.
Me sitting there in her arms,
half-understanding what everyone
was losing their mind about.

Now that I'm older,
I see why millions watch
with bated breath
and get sloppy drunk on the drama.

TWO HOURS FLY BY

like a no-look pass
and Camilo still hasn't returned.
I need to get out of here.
It's weird being in Camilo's place without him,
his grandfather asleep in the other room.
The old man has no idea who I am,
can't ever remember meeting me.
But Camilo said to just leave him be,
so I do.

Since I've read all I can read
and watched all the soap opera
I can stand, I go out for a stroll.

Not before grabbing the
17 bucks Camilo rejected.

I walk and walk,
my book in hand.

Don't really know
why I brought it.

I feel at home on these
unpredictable streets.
More than I thought I would.

I pass the jewelry vendors
and hat sellers
and the old men and women
who push wooden carts
filled with mounds of fresh fruit.

Kids zoom past on bikes,
with the wind in their hair.
Red-and-white hibiscus flowers
pop out like they've got something to say.

Colombian flags sway in the sky.
Laughter spills out onto the roads.
I stop at a bench to read a few pages.

A man with a Rambo knife
struts by, he talks to himself and slings
curse words at the breeze.

A drop of rain falls on my hand.
It rained in Macondo, too, for almost five years.
I'll need to take a taxi back soon.

I SPEND MOST OF MY DOUGH

on a handmade
bag for Daniela.
A purple-and lime-
green mochila,
the brightest thing
I've ever seen.
I use the rest
of the cash
to buy mango
with salt and lime juice,
the tastiest mango
I've ever had.
I'm glad Camilo
left the cash behind.
I'd be mango-less
without it.

I RIDE BACK TO MY TÍA'S HOUSE

and on the way, pass a pink building
with a sign that says *second chances*.
The driver, a man with bronze, leathery skin
and a warm, chip-toothed smile,
tells me it's a prison. A prison that doubles
as a restaurant. Inmates serve the public
while serving their jail time.
It's run by a Michelin-star chef who
likes to dance the conga.

Good wine. Top-notch ceviche de pescado,
the man says. I can hardly believe my ears.
A second chance is a second dance.

ALL THIS PRISON TALK

and now I can't help
but picture myself
behind bars in
an overcrowded
Colombian jail
with two cellmates.
Camilo and the man
who killed my father
with his truck.
In my daydream,
the three of us
are serving life sentences.
We spend our days reading
books with frayed pages
from the library
and doing pushups
to be more muscular
than the others.
The killer always wins
because he's older,
stronger, and wiser.

I'VE HEARD OF EX-CONVICTS WHO

have spent so much time in jail,
they don't know how to function
when they rejoin society.
They've gotten so used to
being barked at, told when
to eat and when to shower
and sleep that freedom feels
like a job they don't want.

On the outside, some can't find
work or a home or a place to belong,
so they end up right back in a cell,
like slabs of beef in a meat locker.
Prison gives them everything they need:
food, shelter, a schedule, and a community
who accepts them. It's a reverse
    second chance.

WHEN I WALK IN, THEY'RE EATING

bandeja paisa
in the dining room.
What's left of Papi sits
on the piano bench.
But there is no music
left to be made.
His time inside the urn
is coming to an end.

If you don't know,
bandeja paisa is
Colombia's national dish.
It's a hearty combination
of protein and carbs.

A traditional platter consists of:
Colombian sausage,
ground beef,
white rice,
red beans,
fried pork belly,
arepa,
plantains,
avocado,
and a fried egg—
always a fried egg—
on top.

It's a whole lot,
which is why it's
thought of as a heart
attack on a plate.
Love it
at your own risk,
or leave it alone—
your loss.

THE SUN SETS OVER CARTAGENA

like the sky exploding
into a thousand colors.

It kisses the horizon
making shades of
red, blue, and yellow.

From my tía's couch,
I watch the day
fade like ink on paper.

I stare at the urn.
The urn stares back at me.
I'm ready for this
to be over and done.

HEARTBREAK IS

an emptiness that lingers like cigar smoke.
Abandoned books and ignored calls.

Is
staring into space
and watching movies with the sound off.

Is
barely touched peanut butter sandwiches
and the same three songs on the radio.

Is
denial breaking bread with anger.
Scrolling social media for signs of others in misery.

Is
afternoons in bed with blankets over your head.
The tiniest memories flooding back like peace after a storm.

HOME IS

a feeling that warms your stomach.

Is more than the made-up lines
that separate people and nations.

Is a moving target that
twists and folds,
like sharp objects you can't
bring in your carry-on.

Home is and was
and can be
whatever
and wherever
you want to find it,
if you look
hard enough.

MY MIND DRIFTS TO

how different life
would have been
had I grown up here.

                              Half-naked bike rides with Papi.

Chasing pigeons with Daniela around Plaza de Bolívar.

            Hamburgers with Ma at La Pepita on Calle de los Puntales.

Weekly scoops of mint chocolate chip from Gelateria Paradiso.

            Wars of words with Papi's friends' kids whose dads he
                              may or may not have
                              punked.
                    When they were our age.

Sun-drunk summers in Bocagrande.

                                        Good music.

Forever dancing.

                                        And me,

in my room every night,

recording it all
like a scribe
on clean white sheets.

I MISS I MISS I MISS

my friends.

I miss I miss
my bed.

I miss I miss
my room.

(My posters, my LED lights, my record player.)

I miss I miss
my fish, goldie hawn 1 and goldie hawn 2.

I miss I miss
gas-station taquitos and slushies giving me brain freeze.

I miss I miss
Ma's memory foam pillow I sneak from time to time.

I miss I miss
balling with the usual suspects after school.

I miss I miss
Papi's bookshelves that contained worlds both known and
        unknown.

I miss
I miss
I miss not having to miss what was there all along.

DEVON ONCE TOLD ME

that even though he was a baby
when his twin sister died,
he has always felt like a
part of him was missing.

Like a piece of him had also
died with her, his twin, his ace,
the one he shared his mom's belly with
for nine months.

He told me that baby twins
share a language between them
that nobody else can speak.

They're like soulmates
before they enter a world
that will do its best
to break them   apart.

BROTHERS FROM ANOTHER
MOTHER EARTH

This is the longest I've gone
without kicking it with

Devon and Hector.
The longest I've gone
in a long time without

games of horse
dirty jokes
lunchroom slap-boxing
trading playlists
made-up handshakes
dollar milkshakes

after school with my can't-replace
brothers from another
mother and father.

A NEW SCHOOL YEAR IS NOT FAR OFF

and I don't know what to make of it.
Maybe I'm not supposed to make anything of it.
I wish I could let myself enjoy the summer
without the thought of junior year
lurking like a thief.
But then I wouldn't be me.
All I know is that every school year starts off the same.
After you've worn all of your new fits,
which only takes about a week, if that,
it's basically downhill.

Besides lunch and gym,
everything else is like

mental, emotional prison.
I doubt we will read any
García Márquez, which
by itself could maybe save
the whole year.
Or not.

I WONDER

What/How
Devon and Hector
are doing now

Which
of the Cadenas has cried
the most gallons of tears

Why
God made life
so fragile and temporary

What/How
Daniela is thinking
at this exact second

Which
city I love more,
Miami or Cartagena

Why
Camilo

is
coughing
up
blood
again

I NOW HAVE TWO COPIES

of ONE HUNDRED YEARS OF SOLITUDE.

Camilo spotted
a Spanish edition
at a secondhand bookshop
and snagged it for me.

It was published in 1991.
The cover features a
strange-looking tree
in the foreground
with birds flying around it
and mountains behind.

It's about time I learn to read,
and to live,
as my father read
and lived.

In two languages.
Finding myself
at home
in both.

TODAY MAY BE THE LAST DAY WITH CAMILO

. . . .

. . . .

. . . .

SNAP OUT OF IT,

Camilo says.
I say, *I'm here.*

He says, *Do you realize,*
how much you daydream?

I never thought about
it, I lie through my teeth.

Exactly, he says.

I shout back, *Oh,*
you're one to talk!
You're in space more
than the asteroids
that orbit the sun.

IT IS THE BEGINNING OF THE END

The beginning of the end of hangs with my new friend
The beginning of the end of learning more about Gabo in
        his resting place

The beginning of the end of exploring the city by taxi
The beginning of the end of pan de queso on Colombian sidewalks
The beginning of the end of falling more in love with the clopping
        of horse-drawn carriages

Hopefully not the end of dreaming in another tongue
Hopefully not the end of the rest of my life

YESTERDAY, CAMILO BOUGHT ME

a pocketknife with my name
engraved on the handle.

I had told him that my knife,
which Papi gave me for my tenth birthday,
was confiscated at the airport on the way here.
I'd forgotten it was in my backpack
buried under my book, some clothes,
and a second pair of shoes.
The TSA man looked at me stone cold
and tossed my Old Timer
into a bin with a bundle of trash:
creams, hair gels.
A half-empty bottle of rum.

*To the tune of 99 bottles of beer on the wall

♪ *Half-empty bottle of rum in the bin.* ♪

It never feels good to have something
you love taken from you,
whether it's a blade or a soulmate.
A reminder that some things
can never be replaced.

WHAT IS A SODA WORTH?

Drinking a Colombiana with Camilo is more fun than YMCA
games or walking around Bayfront Park by my lonesome as
beats boom from passing cars.

Drinking a Colombiana with Camilo and getting swept up in
the rhythm of his stories as he plays with the zipper on his Fila

windbreaker is more fun than hearing my neighbors fight over
nonsense like who said what about who.

Drinking a Colombiana with Camilo and thinking to myself

It feels like I've known him all my life

but not saying it out loud is fun, because a picture of friendship
is worth a thousand unspoken words.

I ASK CAMILO ABOUT THE PHOTO

The one of García Márquez
with the busted-up eye.
Many years ago,
so goes the story,
Gabo was mixed up in a feud
with Mario Vargas Llosa,
another South American writer.
The why is hazy
(some say wives were involved),
but the nitty gritty is that Vargas Llosa
landed a clean right hook
at a film premiere in Mexico City.
Gabo fell, bloodied up,
his glasses splitting
on the bridge of his nose.
Someone gave him
a piece of raw meat
to help with the swelling.

Years later, in 2010,
Vargas Llosa won
the Nobel Prize in Literature.
Definitely not the
Nobel Peace Prize.

CAMILO ON MAGIC MUSHROOMS

Camilo unlocks the portal
to who knows where
and steps inside.
Some wonderland
in his mind's eye.
Physically he is here
but mentally he's on a trip,
where worlds burst
open and worry
leaves the body.

He's exploring the ins
and the outs
of the unknown, he says.
Tells me what he sees
as he sees it.

Revolving doors
and candy-colored peacocks
coming out of the walls.
He goes on these trips
occasionally,

on his days off,
when he needs
clarity on something.

A level of consciousness
only psychedelic drugs can give.
There is no worrying
or stressing, Camilo says,
no questioning or answering.
There is only being.

. . . .

He looks out
of the living room window
and spots my father
in the distance.
Yes, my father.
Describes his kind eyes
and calm spirit.
His hair is wavy
and thick like a lion's.

Papi stands tall
in the void
dressed in all black.
Covered in light.
He stares at Camilo
warmly, like he would
a faithful friend.

Papi reaches above
his head for two stars
and throws them to Camilo
like spiked frisbees.

These are for Marcos,
Papi says,
without speaking.
His eyes say,
Please give these to my son.

Camilo places the
two stars
in my hands.
I don't see anything,
but Camilo is convinced
I am holding them.

Suddenly, a peace
comes over me.
It covers me from
top to bottom,
like a healing,
calming presence.

This is why
I came to Cartagena.
And this is why
I met Camilo.

PAPI'S ONLY TATTOO

sat on his chest
above his right pec.
It was a large ship
with three yellow
flowers in front.

Today I browse Camilo's shelf,
like I've done now many times,
at the various editions
of ONE HUNDRED YEARS OF SOLITUDE.

Among this collection I see what must have
been Papi's tattoo inspiration,
which meant enough to him that
he chose to put it on his body for keeps.

It's the same image from the
cover of the first edition.
Camilo believes the cover art comes
from one of the book's early paragraphs.

He grabs it and reads it to me,
something about:

Ferns and palm trees,
the silent morning light,
an enormous ship,
a forest of flowers.

I LACE UP MY KICKS TO SHOOT BASKETS

up the street. Camilo says
he's going out
with his grandfather.
He sets down the duffle
bag he's holding
and gives me a tight hug,
which for some reason
feels like *goodbye*.
He tells me to look
both ways on the
winding road of life
and we laugh,
reminded of the time he nearly
vehicular manslaughtered me
that day at the airport.
Camilo, my mom will be here
in a few hours, so don't take forever.
We bump fists and the two
disappear out the door.
Camilo starts up the taxi and
cranks the stereo,
heavy metal blaring
like a storm is coming.
I walk out dribbling the ball
and yell *Hurry up!* as he rushes off.
It feels too much like
　　have a nice life.

IT'S A HOT ONE IN CARTAGENA

Miami in July level hot.
Oozing melted rock hot.
Fever hot.
Ghost pepper hot.
Ma's morning cafecito hot.
Cold as my jump shot hot.
DMX *It's Dark and Hell Is Hot* hot.
Heat wave in Gabo's Macondo where
men and beasts go ballistic and
birds attack houses hot.
Too hot for TV.
Papi's invisible stars in my hands hot.
So hot I return to Camilo's
house after 10 minutes.

I AM SPOOKED

by the sight
of a boy peeking
through the window
like a private detective.
We make eye contact
and he motions for me
to go outside. I immediately
know that it's Fernando,
Camilo's former friend,
and now enemy.
Our enemy. I clock a steak

knife with a blade at least
four inches long
in his belt and wonder
to myself if this is how
my story ends.

I walk up to him but don't let
my face tell what I know.

Fernando: *Where is Marcos?*

Me: *I don't know.*

Fernando: *When will he return?*

Me: . . . *I'm not sure.*

Fernando: *What are you good for?*

Me: *To be honest, I don't know that either.*

He looks at me,
visibly irritated,
and leaves.

My story
will go on.
My reading
will continue.

I FIND A NOTE FROM CAMILO

on page 146.

It's folded in half
with an arrow
pointing to a 4-word sentence,
which Camilo underlined.
It reads, *They became great friends*.

The passage is about
Colonel Aureliano Buendía
and the mayor of Macondo—
General José Raquel Moncada—
who struck a friendship
even though they were from
rival political parties.

Camilo's note:

Marcos, thank you for being a great friend to me.
I found out that the boy who was hit
is in critical care and is not expected to
recover. I don't know what to do just yet.
But I cannot let hate and bitterness swallow me whole.
My grandfather still needs me, so we have to disappear for now,
until I can find a place where he will be safe,
can find a way to clear my lungs of this cancer.
I know you will go back to Miami soon.
Please do not worry for me.
And please give my love to your mother.

Marcos, I don't think we will see each other again,
but I hope you will keep the stars that your father
gave to me to give you. Remember him, but also remember
to live. Burn hot with the light of his love for you
and do not be condemned to 100 years of solitude.
Life can be a tough dance, and a sometimes dark one.
But it can still be beautiful. Thank you for helping me
to see and feel and understand this again.
Now is your time to reach for another beginning.
Listen, every human needs a thing.
That thing that makes them come alive,
And that makes life more fun and meaningful.
Too many people don't have a thing, Marcos.
And that's a big problem. Find your thing
and you will never be empty.
Your dear friend forever and always,
Camilo.

I JUST WANT

to tell him
to his face
he's one of
the best
friends
I've ever had.

I want him
to know that
in one week
he changed how

I see myself.
See my father.
See my countries.

I hope he
can be free
and have someone
nearby that he
can confide in.
Like a brother.
I never got
to tell him
that secret he
asked for. Maybe
that's reason alone
to find each
other again,
someday.

PAPI / GABO / CAMILO

You left me
and us holding on
by a thread
in a world
without you
and without
your magic.

But we will
always have

what you left behind,
your words
and your letters,
and they will age
with love

like a recipe
passed down,
multiplying
its magic.

JUST A FEELING

I don't know if it's
where we were born
or who we were born to
or the books we read
or the movies we watched
or the music we listened to
or the food we ate
or if it's a combination
of all these things—
but in some spooky way
it feels like the four of us
are shades of the same person.

I READ AND READ

and read some more.
The book that floats

above every other.
Drinking the long
sentences slowly now
as they jump
from human to human
and generation to generation.
I sip water.
Breathe in.
Breathe out.
Look out the window
between pages.
Breathe in.
Breathe out.
Read between the lines.
Breathe in.
Breathe out.

CHERRY RED

I gather my things

and shoot one last glance

at Camilo's kingdom,

this house that was a home.

Parked out front is a glossy red BMW

convertible, a car that Papi used to love.

Kool-Aid red. Red as a rose, red as strawberries and ladybugs.

Red as the flame in your heart

when you find out a girl you dig

is crushing on you back.

I look at Ma, at my tía Norma,

and then over at Daniela who's all

smiles in the backseat.

Ma says, *I rented it just for the day,*

so we can cruise Cartagena in style.

AS WE PULL OUT OF THE DRIVEWAY

I see two police cars
driving in our direction,
lights flashing but no sirens.
They zip past us and Ma says,
I wonder what that is about.
I shrug like I'm clueless,
but I think I know where
they're going and what it's about.

Is this it? Did Camilo sense that
someone was coming? Why didn't he warn me?
Did he trust me enough to know I wouldn't panic?

Before we turn the corner, I yell at Ma
louder than I've ever yelled at anyone.

Stop the car!

Ma slams hard on the pedal
like Camilo did that time
he nearly killed us
and the arepa vendor.

I watch as the two police cars
pass the house, headed elsewhere.
For now, relief.

BEACH CRIES

Me and Ma sit on the sand,
a water urn with Papi's
ashes beside us on a towel.

Daniela and my tía splash
waves along the shore,
their pants rolled up to the knees.

Ma says, *In our many years together,
I saw your father cry exactly six times.*

When I walked down the aisle
When two of his close friends died five months apart
When Colombia beat Mexico to win their first Copa América title
When you were born
When your sister was born
When García Márquez died

Ma leaves for the bathroom
and I sit alone, running sand
through my fingers.

I HAVE NOT PRAYED IN AGES

but if I were to pray,
I would ask all of heaven
to hug my mother.
To hold her
for an hour straight.
To teach her spirit
how to move on, somehow,
despite losing the only man
she ever loved.
The only man
she ever kissed.
The only man I watched
pull her hair back
to help her throw up
that time she drank
too much rum
at her 40th birthday party.

HE WAS ONLY 44

Tough as beef jerky.
Compassionate.
Sometimes guarded.
Mostly let you see his full heart.
Loved to tease Ma.
Lived to protect those he loved.
Never put hands on me in anger.
Had a glint in his eyes that told you
when he was serious.
Took his coffee black as midnight.
Rarely finished his coffee because he'd get
distracted by a song and have to warm it up
in the microwave
again and again.
Was a cocktail of contradictions,
like his only son.
Only 44.
He was.

SOME THINGS ARE BETTER LEFT

Some words   are better left unsaid.

Some messages   are better left unread.

Some hunger pangs   are better left unfed.

Some butters   are better left unspread.

Some wounds   are better left unbled.

Some people   are better left undead.

AGAINST, AGAIN AND AGAIN

Against the grain
Against my will
Against my better judgement

Against the clock
Against the current
A race against time

Against the law
Against them, us
Back against the wall

Me against the world
Rage against the machine
A house divided against itself falls

I want to stand
against whatever
is against life.

I, Marcos Cadena,
am for life,
against all odds.

A FAMILY OF THREE

We used to be four, now we are three.
I used to be just Marcos, now I am me.

She used to be little Daniela, now she's going to high school.
Ma used to be a wife, now she's a widow.

We're staring at the ocean in silence.
We're the same, but different than we were.

We used to be four,
                            now we must learn to be more
                                                        with less.

It's that or die trying.

FLOWERS FOR THE DEAD

Ma returns from the bathroom
with a bouquet of yellow roses
she bought on the street.
She says that on García Márquez's
87th birthday, a month before
he passed away,
a crowd had gathered outside
of his home in Mexico
to sing "Mañanitas,"
the traditional Mexican birthday song.

García Márquez stood
outside the door smiling
at the people and holding
a bouquet of yellow roses
they brought for him
  like these.

REMEMBER TO REMEMBER

I hope to always
remember this summer.
Though I know
most of it
will stick
like Elmer's
glue,
I'm sure
there are details
I will forget
like a sucky
report card
because as I mentioned
once in a poem,
or whatever you want to call it,
I never remember   my dreams.

I AM NEARING THE END OF THE NOVEL

and every third or fourth page
looking up the definitions for

words I don't know.

Rancor, disenchantment, motley, taciturn.

Something about how certain words
feel and taste and sound.

Like cashmere.
Like caramel.
Like a melody.

Something about how the translator
chose them so carefully,

saying what needed to be said
as they bridged two worlds.

Picking the perfect ones
from an endless bundle of language.

This one fits here,
that one is tailor-made for there.

The sky is turning a soft shade of orange.

I know it's almost time
to disappear   from here.

THE FOUR OF US

look out toward infinity,
taking it all in.
The warm Caribbean
water shines like crystal.
Ma sets down the urn
on the surface
of the water and steps back.
We four watch as a light wind
pushes it further and further
away before finally sinking,
returning Papi to the city he loved
more than any other.

We are here to see about the future.

PAPI . . .

I hate that it took
losing you
for me to find
and accept myself.
But even if I can't
touch you, you will
always be here.
Because your Cartagena
is here. And
Gabo is here.
You have no choice

but to carry us,
to carry me.
And I will
carry you also,
until my heart gives in
like the final chorus.

CARTAGENA ...

I hate that it took
losing Papi

for me
to know your breeze

against my face.
Now we're linked

forever, like championship rings
and your air of mystery.

I'll be back soon enough,
even if it means doing

it my way. Cartagena,
you can bet on that.

WE MAKE A PIT STOP

to see Papi's childhood home.
It's a 1,000-square-foot apartment
the color of canned peaches on the
bottom floor of a three-story walk-up.

This is where Papi took his first steps.
Where he said his first words.
Where he first encountered the universe
Gabo created, never to be the same.

Kids run around playing soccer
and cracking jokes, the way I
bet Papi and his friends did trying to
one-up each other to impress girls.

Papi told me they once spray-painted
the side of this building with swear words
only to get caught in the act and have to
make the walls and their hearts clean again.

EN ROUTE TO THE AIRPORT

I stare into every cab that passes.
I see no teenager behind the wheel
of any of them.
No sign of that dented bumper
or my favorite outlaw
who could be all the way in
Barranquilla or Medellín by now.

Daniela babbles on from the back seat
but I can't hear her over the radio.
Ma turns to me and makes a funny face,
pokes at my side with her finger.
She looks very young and very beautiful.

Is a life waiting to be lived.
Spotless like the page before the poem.

RED LETTERS ON A BOARDED-UP STOREFRONT READ

LO ÚNICO QUE GUARDAS
ES LO QUE PUEDES RECORDAR

THE ONLY THING YOU KEEP
IS WHAT YOU CAN REMEMBER

I AM THAT I AM

an open heart and hand.
Cartagena has etched
its magic in me.
Magic that will
burn longer
than the images
of sun and sky

found in postcards
and travel posters.

Tonight, I will dream
of a city
where magic
is still possible.

A city of ghosts,
banana trees,
and birds of flame.
Of a man named
José Arcadio who inherits
his father's strength,

as I have.
And I will remember
the dream when I wake up
in my own bed.

It will feel like
a baptism, or
   like a fist unclenching.

DEPARTURE

The agent scans
my ticket. I look
at my seat
number before
crumpling it into
a ball and
tossing it into
the wastebasket.

My last jumpshot
in Colombia.

I don't know
what tomorrow
will bring, but I can
bank on the facts:

Three rights make a left.
Ball is life.
And a father is a thing that you lose.

NOW, IF I COULD JUST CONVINCE THE PILOT

that ball is life I'd politely
ask him to take
a few detours.

We'd pick up Devon and Hector
and hit every court on every continent
and get fancy like the Harlem Globetrotters.

Asia, Africa, and North America
would get the business.

South America, Europe, and Australia
would feel our wrath.

Not even the polar bears in Antarctica
would be safe, as I drop threes like clockwork
and try not to die from frostbite.

IN THIS POEM

everyone lives.
Nobody dies
and everyone

    stays awake.

In this dream,
everybody lives.
No one dies
and everybody

    wakes up

and remembers what they dreamt.

INSTRUCTIONS ON MOVING ON

Gabo, I hate that it took so long
for me to discover what you created

for us, but I'm thankful that I did.
Your story has ended

and Papi's story has ended,
and something else has to begin.

I pore over its last words
and close the book.

Macondo has been wrecked
by the wind of the apocalypse.

Time has run out
for the Buendía family.

I've processed my new reality
and made space for something else to grow,

like a stubborn rose out
of a crack in the cement.

PREPARE FOR TAKEOFF

Turns out there's some
of the summer left.

I'll definitely give
the YMCA a fair go.

That should help fill the days
before Devon and Hector reappear.

But first there's this three-hour flight.
Ma dozes off. Daniela zones out

to Top 40 hits on Ma's phone.
I wonder what Camilo is up to.

I hope he finds what he doesn't know he
needs. I hope the fuzz crack the case and learn who hit

that boy so my friend can live
in peace in his, Gabo's, and Papi's Cartagena.

In my Cartagena.
Three long hours.

There's nothing better to do so I reopen
the book and start again at the beginning.

When I first saw it on Papi's shelf
that day, I was intrigued, but unsure.

(It seems so long ago.)

Now I know why Camilo calls it
The Story Behind The Story.

The one that lives an
afterlife in your mind.

The truth is, Papi's presence
has haunted this novel
from the moment I picked it up.
The one I'm reading,
    and the one I've been living.

From here forward I pledge
to only look ahead.
To run or fly like hell
in the direction of whatever is good
and do whatever it is I wish
with this second chance on earth.

REVELATION 21, THE REMIX

Then, Camilo said, I saw a new Miami and a new Cartagena, as the first ones were chewed up and swallowed by rising sea levels. **2** *I saw the Holy City, the new Macondo, coming down from the clouds, prepared like a bride beautifully dressed for her husband.* **3** *And I heard a thunderous voice from the throne saying, Look! Gabo's dwelling place is now among the people, and all will know that Camilo is innocent—he is a simple taxi driver with simple dreams of freedom.* **4** *From now on, the voice continued, there will be no more death or mourning or false accusations or crying or pain, for the old ways are gone and everything is so fresh and so clean, clean.* **5** *I am the Gabo.* **6** *The Alpha and the Omega, the Beginning and the End. To the hungry I will give stories to eat.* **7** *Those who are victorious will enjoy true nourishment, and I will be their Maestro and they will be my children.* **8** *But the cowardly, the mean, the annoying, the thieves, the murderers, the idolaters, liars, and all those who double dribble—they will be sent to the dreadful lake of lukewarm Coca Cola. This is the second death. But those who are good and merciful and practice kindness and can cook up a half-decent haiku on the spot are those whose names are written in Gabo's book of life. The only book that matters.*

CAN YOU HEAR IT? PLEASE TELL ME, CAN ANYONE HEAR IT?

That is the sound
of my dry bones

clicking, mending,
rising up to take their place.

ACKNOWLEDGMENTS

Thank you to my family, my everything; big props to my agent Alex Slater for your trust and your guidance; all my gratitude to Alexandra Aceves, a dream of an editor whose sharp eye and sound mind helped bring this vision to life; un abrazo to my tío Carlos who introduced me to the work of Gabriel García Márquez at his apartment in Cali, Colombia when I was 16; to the good ghost of Gabo for fanning the flame; and finally, thank you to the givers, and the receivers, of second chances the world over.